Jessie caught up with me before I could reach the front door.

"What's the matter with you?" she asked, grabbing my arm and spinning me around.

"I don't know. I guess I just don't like working with a bully. I kept waiting for you to take out a baseball bat and threaten to smash his kneecaps."

"Well, I'm not too crazy about being with someone who pussyfoots around everyone like he's afraid of his own shadow," she shot back.

I took a deep breath, counted to ten, then to twenty and tried to sound reasonable. "All I'd like is for you to use a little tact, a smidgen of diplomacy, instead of pretending that you're a steamroller and everyone else is a worm. Trying to scare information out of people isn't always the way to go."

She went out the door. I almost had to run to keep up, but even if our partnership was over, I needed a ride home. It was too far to walk.

Lou Dunlop: PRIVATE EYE

GLEN EBISCH

CROSSWINDS

New York • Toronto
Sydney • Auckland
Manila

For my wife.

"Stopping by Woods on a Snowy Evening" from
THE POETRY OF ROBERT FROST edited by
Edward Connery Lathem.
Copyright 1923, © 1969 by Holt, Rinehart and
Winston. Copyright 1951 by Robert Frost. Reprinted by
permission of Henry Holt and Company.

First publication June 1987

ISBN 0-373-98002-7

Copyright © by Glen Ebisch

Printed in the U.S.A.

RL 5.6, IL age 10 and up

GLEN EBISCH received his Ph.D. in philosophy from Columbia University and currently teaches at Elms College in Chicopee, Massachusetts. He is the author of a number of academic articles and a short story for young adults. In his fiction he admits to being influenced by the work of Dashiell Hammett and Raymond Chandler. He frequently spends his summers admiring the Victorian houses in Cape May, New Jersey. His hobbies include reading, jogging and basketball.

Dear Reader:

Welcome to Crosswinds! We will be publishing four books a month, written by renowned authors and rising new stars. You will note that under our Crosswinds logo we are featuring a special line called Keepsake, romantic novels that are sure to win your heart.

We hope that you will read Crosswinds books with pleasure, and that from time to time you will let us know just what you think of them. Your comments and suggestions will help us to keep Crosswinds at the top of your reading list.

Nancy Jackson

Senior Editor
CROSSWINDS BOOKS

One

The school year is really messed up, you know. There are only three months from the beginning of school to Christmas, with all sorts of holidays thrown in, but after you come back there are still seven more months to go—seven long, cold months. Oh, sure, there's usually a week off in March, when the weather is lousy unless you're rich enough to go to the Bahamas or somewhere. But from January to June, everybody in school is just counting down the days until the summer.

All this is kind of an excuse, I guess, for why I was daydreaming in English class. I had a seat near

the window—I always try to get one there so I have
something to look at when things get boring—and
the teacher was going on about this writer Henry
David Thoreau living in a shack he built near Wal-
den Pond.

Eleventh-grade English is supposed to cover
American writers, but they never seem to get out of
the 1800s. Even if they did, they probably wouldn't
talk about my favorite: Raymond Chandler. He
wrote in the 1930s and 1940s, and his main character was Philip Marlowe, this real tough private
eye. Marlowe wasn't afraid of anything. Cops,
hoods, guys with money: nothing stopped him
from solving a case. He just didn't worry.

My problem, or at least one of them, is that I
worry all the time. I worry about the pimple on my
chin, about failing Algebra, about not getting into
college, about my father being down on me. I worry
about whether girls like me or not, about whether
I'll do something stupid and look like a jerk in front
of everybody, about being too tall and thin. And
even though I'm only seventeen, I worry about
having to die someday. Like I told you, I worry a
lot. Marlowe had it easy.

But I wasn't thinking about Marlowe in English
class. I was looking out the window and trying to
imagine what it must have been like in Thoreau's

time or even earlier, when only the Indians were here. I mentally took out the split-levels across the street and replaced them with some trees and tepees. Winter in a tent. Those Indians must have looked forward to spring even more than I do.

"Louis Dunlop! How much did Thoreau spend to build his cabin?" Mrs. Kasterson's voice came out of the present like fingernails on a blackboard.

My eyes snapped back to the front of the room, and I felt my face start to get warm from the neck up. Kasterson had that superior smile on her face that she gets when she knows she's caught someone.

"If you want to know the price of real estate, lady, buy a newspaper," Marlowe would have answered. I said nothing and got redder as a few kids began to laugh. Bill Watkins, the class jerk, sounded like a hyena, as usual.

Finally the witch got tired of making me suffer in silence. "I've noticed that you spend quite a bit of your time staring out the window, Louis."

"That's because your class would drive a minister to drink," Marlowe whispered in the back of my mind.

"What's out there that's so interesting?" she asked.

I didn't answer. What was there to say? By now a few more kids were laughing. It seemed to me that they were rolling in the aisles.

That was when she made her mistake.

"Since you find it so difficult to concentrate on what I'm saying when you are seated near the window, Louis, I'm going to move you to the empty seat in the second row," she said, pointing to the seat as though I were blind or really stupid.

The laughter stopped as if someone had turned off the sound in the room. Even Watkins shut up. She was moving me to *the seat*. It had been Cathy McKenna's desk until she had disappeared in November, and no one had used it since. Although we didn't talk about it much, everybody hoped that someday Cathy would be sitting there again. Now Kasterson was as good as saying it would never happen.

She realized her mistake, and her eyes moved nervously around the room. "Louis!" she barked. "Move! This very instant!"

Trying to seem as casual as possible, considering that my face probably looked like a tomato, I picked up my books and walked over to Cathy's old desk. I slumped down in the seat and glanced over to my right. Jessie Phillips gave me a small smile. At least she wasn't laughing, so I flashed her my best Marlowe grin—the look of a guy who's seen everything and done it all. She just looked puzzled. Sometimes style is wasted on kids.

Kasterson picked up the lesson again, and I paid attention for a while, although I was kind of ashamed of myself for doing it. I should have walked out of the room after telling her to stuff it. Anyway, Kasterson was right about one thing, I couldn't see much out the window from my new seat. So when she turned her back to write Thoreau's expense account on the board, I started to read the top of the desk.

There were the usual four-letter words, an infantile drawing of a giant joint with smoke coming out the end and a picture of two stick figures doing something weird; one was labeled Kasterson. I started to smile but stopped when I saw a drawing of a little heart on the right-hand corner of the desk. Inside the heart was written Cathy and ___ . The second name was too smudged to read, as if maybe she'd had second thoughts about writing it down at all and rubbed it out.

I felt someone watching me and glanced around. Jessie again. Okay, sweetheart, I thought in my best Marlowe manner, look all you want; there's no charge. And I sat back with my arms folded as though I really didn't care.

As soon as English was over, Jessie reached over and grabbed my arm tightly. "I want to talk to you! In the hall! Now!" she whispered fiercely.

I nodded and just managed to stop myself from rubbing my arm to get the circulation started again.

"Private investigators have to get used to strange women wanting to see them alone," Marlowe whispered in my mind.

Yeah, I thought nervously, already worried.

Out in the hall, she pointed, and we began walking. I started to say something, but she motioned me to be quiet. I had never walked down the hall next to a girl like Jessie. She was wearing a blue denim jacket over a blue work shirt, and her really tight, faded jeans were tucked into a pair of black boots with high heels. The clacking of the heels on the tiles in the hall sounded like a regiment of Nazis goose-stepping. Her light blond hair and the miniature bicycle chain she wore for a necklace completed the picture. Otherwise—a big otherwise—she was kind of cute.

She moved me into a secluded corner across from the clinic. The door was open, and inside I could see the nurse quieting down a mob of kids. There must have been twenty of them. They looked as though they had just come through a war. At least half were on crutches, some had an arm or leg in a cast and others were claiming that they should have. A few were doing a pretty good imitation of trying to throw up.

"How many want me to call your parents to pick you up?" the nurse shouted.

Nobody moved. It was like they were made out of stone.

"How many of you want to go home?" she asked. Everyone except for Psychosomatic Sally raised a hand or cast. Sally's had a bellyache since third grade and spends more time in the clinic than in class. She's almost an assistant nurse now. Someday she'll probably become a doctor and make a fortune.

The nurse groaned and shut the door.

"Are you listening to me, Dunlop?" Jessie snapped. With those boots on she was almost as tall as I am, which is about six feet one inch, and she was standing closer to me than a girl usually does.

"So what do you think?" she asked.

I stared. "About what?"

"Watch my lips this time, and try to keep up," she ordered. "You saw Cathy's heart on the desk. What do you make of it?"

I tried to look thoughtful. "Not much. Maybe Cathy had a boyfriend."

"Why would she rub his name out?" Jessie shot back.

"I don't know. Maybe she changed boyfriends or decided she wanted him to be a secret."

"Yeah, and maybe someone else wants to keep it a secret," Jessie said grimly.

"What do you mean?" Her remark had the sound of trouble to it, and that was something I wanted to stay out of.

"Look, I had three classes with Cathy, and on her desk in each one is a heart with the guy's name rubbed out. Now maybe this guy had something to do with her disappearance, so he's trying to hide his name."

"Maybe," I said, unconvinced.

Jessie looked at me as if I were slow-witted. "Did you have any classes with Cathy other than English?"

I tried to remember. It's funny how quickly after someone is gone that you forget she was ever there.

"Yeah, we were in Home Economics together," I answered.

"Do you know how to cook?" she asked out of the blue, giving me a sidelong glance.

"My father works strange hours and my mother is dead, so sometimes I do the cooking."

"Oh," she said a little more softly. "But they don't have desks in home ec, do they?"

"No, only tables. And look, the police have probably been over all this stuff already."

"The police." She sounded sarcastic. "They didn't even come around to look at her desk. They've already made up their minds that she was just some crazy kid who got picked up along the road hitchhiking or ran away to the city."

"Maybe she did," I suggested timidly.

"Cathy was a little strange in some ways, but not dumb. I don't think she would get into a car with some weird guy, and she seemed too happy to run away from home. She really liked her folks," Jessie added in a tone of near amazement.

I wondered what Jessie meant by "a little strange." If Jessie thought Cathy was odd, she must have been a straightjacket case. I didn't have any intention of getting involved with some lunatic who wanted to go looking for another one.

I edged out into the hall. "Look, if I don't go, I'll be late for class. Anybody could have grabbed her off the street. It happens all the time. You seem sure she was kidnapped by somebody that she was going out with, or even," I added hesitantly, "by someone here at school."

"All I'm saying is that this heart business is funny," Jessie grumbled.

"So why wait three months to follow up on it?" I asked impatiently. "You sound like you've got it all figured out."

She bit her lip as if she wanted to get angry but changed her mind. "I didn't know what to do, or even if it was any of my business. What could I do? Go to the police, tell her parents? I don't even know them. And it's not like I've got real proof. But Cathy was sort of a friend, and it's been eating at me that I didn't do anything. I told a couple of other people, but they didn't want to be bothered. You seem different, and I guess I figured that the two of us together, you know, might be able to find out something."

She looked right at me with her dark brown eyes, and I heard someone saying, "Okay, maybe I'll check out the home ec room tomorrow, and you make a list of places where she used to hang out."

As soon as I recognized that the voice was mine, I wanted to back out, say I was sorry, but my three-month safari to Africa was leaving tomorrow.

But then Jessie gave me a big smile, like this was the best thing that had happened to her in months. "Great! I knew you'd have some good ideas. Here's my phone number if you need to talk to me," she said, scribbling her number on my book cover with a violet magic marker.

So instead of running away, I gave her one of my sophisticated smiles, one eyebrow up and all, and said, "See you tomorrow, Jes." I walked down the hall real slowly—super cool.

"You've just been suckered, kid," Marlowe whispered in my mind.

Shut up! I thought.

Two

By the time I met Eric after school and we started walking home, I had all sorts of doubts about what I'd told Jessie. I knew that if I backed out now, she'd think I was a jerk—a frightened jerk. And why not admit it, I was frightened. Kids don't go around investigating disappearances that could be murders. I'd be more of a jerk to get involved.

Eric looked at me a couple of times as we went along because I wasn't saying much. I knew he was willing to wait until I decided that I needed someone to spill it all out to. I was lucky to have Eric for a friend. You get to know a lot of guys at school, and some you like to go around and do things with, but you can't really talk to most of them. That was the thing about Eric: he listened and had some really good things to say.

As usual, we walked on the sidewalk, then cut off and went along the railroad tracks. Going this way saved me about twenty minutes, and it was kind of interesting walking where nobody much goes. There were all sorts of things thrown along the sides of the tracks: liquor bottles, soup cans, railroad spikes, clothes and sometimes even shoes.

When Eric had first shown me this path, I'd asked him if he thought that being a hobo would be fun, drifting from one place to another without any problems or hassles. Eric thought that the drifting part was fine, but you had to have money to drift in style. He did. His parents were divorced, and he lived with his mother in a section of town about half a mile from my house. But it was a long half mile. My father and I lived in the cheapest part of town, which was still pretty fancy, but where Eric lived was like being in a park. You couldn't see the houses from the street in the summer; the lawns were all neatly trimmed with little circles of dirt around each of the trees and even the birds sitting in the trees looked kind of like they were trained.

Even with all his money, though, Eric wasn't a
snob like some of the rich kids who walked around
with their noses up in the air all the time. He didn't
bring his car to school much because he liked to
walk, and clothes didn't seem to make any difference to him. But I did enjoy being with someone
who had money because he never seemed to worry.
I guess money does that for you. Plus we talked a
lot, and that's not something that I'll do with just
anybody.

On the way home we always stopped at The
Clearing. This was what Eric called a spot that was
away from the tracks a little and not within sight of
any houses. Even in the winter it was pretty well
concealed by evergreens and bushes, and during the
rest of the year, Eric said, it was like a huge green
room, with trees forming the walls and ceiling. We
kept a couple of crates there, and except on the
coldest days, we would stop for a while to sit,
smoke and talk.

As we sat down, I told Eric about Mrs. Kasterson and the window.

"Yeah," he said, his eyes lighting up, "I wonder what it was like around here a hundred and fifty
years ago. It would be really something to travel
back in time to actually see what it was like."

"It may sound stupid," I said, "but I've always worried that, if I traveled back in time, the place where I am now would turn out to be in the middle of a wall or under a lake. You never know what was where you're standing right now."

"You worry a lot. But, you know, there is one way you could be safe, at least if you were only going back a couple of hundred years."

"How's that?"

"Look around for the largest tree you can find and hold on to it as you travel back. Any really big tree was probably here two hundred years ago."

"I suppose you're right," I admitted, impressed and a little envious at how he'd figured that out.

Eric nodded and lit another cigarette from mine. We sat in comfortable silence, smoking and watching the late afternoon sun slant through the trees. Usually I get nervous when I'm in the same room with someone and we're not talking. I'll bring up really weird things: the price of bananas in Costa Rica, inflation, how to cure athlete's foot, anything just to break the silence. But with Eric it was different; we only talked when we had something to say.

It had been like that even the first time Eric Hannah and I had met back in September right after school started. I had walked out to the county park one Saturday and had run into Eric by Baker's Pond. We got to talking about school, sports, traveling and all sorts of stuff. Since he had just moved into town, there were a lot of things he wanted to know. I even told him about a few of my problems, and he listened as if he were really interested. Even though he was my age, in some ways he was more like an adult. I mean, he had thought about things.

Because my high school is really big, it was a couple of months before I got to talk to him much except to say hi in the halls. Then he stopped me one afternoon as I was going home and said he had a great shortcut over to our side of town and asked me if I would like to see it. Now, I guess, we were friends.

"Kasterson's a real jerk," I grumbled, the embarrassment of the morning coming back in a flash. "She always tries to make you look like a fool."

"That's because she's a typical subnormal," said Eric, flicking the ash from his cigarette.

Eric had three categories for people, based on their intelligence, personality and style. Subnormals are not too bright, do stupid things and think they're the coolest people in the world. Normals are regular folks, nothing special either way. Super-normals are smart, always know what they're doing and are always cool.

"Yeah, I guess you're right," I admitted. "There's no point getting mad at her. She can't help being what she is. But sometimes it's hard to remember that."

"I know, but remember, too, that she's got the authority. No matter what retarded thing she does, the principal will back her up," Eric warned.

I figured that Eric was just trying to make me feel good, but I knew he wouldn't have taken that kind of crap from Kasterson. She wouldn't even have tried it with him; somehow even teachers know that there are some kids you can mess with and some you can't.

Since I had already told him about Kasterson, I decided to lay out the whole thing, so I told him about the heart on the desk and my talk with Jessie. "What do you think?" I asked when I was done.

"I can see why the clone of Philip Marlowe would be interested, but I don't think that you've got much of a chance."

"Why not?" I was a little angry because I suspected he was right.

"You know, this isn't a story or some television show. It's real life. Cathy may have run away, or she may be dead, but no matter which, it's a job for the police. You know that. All that can happen is that you'll get into some kind of trouble."

Maybe he was right, but I was disappointed that someone who usually teased me about being cautious wouldn't encourage me to take a chance. Probably he didn't think I could handle it. But I didn't argue; instead I said, "You're right, I guess. Jessie could be all wet, and the police have more than likely checked all this out already."

"Well, if you decide to go ahead with it, let me know, and I'll give you some help if you need it."

I nodded dejectedly, and he gave me a grin. "C'mon, let's start walking. The future is full of things to do and places to see."

We walked along without speaking, and for the first time I was a little uncomfortable. I think it was because, somewhere in my mind during the past five minutes, I had decided that I was going to go ahead and try to find out what happened to Cathy and I wasn't going to tell Eric. I'd show him that I wasn't just pretending to be a detective, and when it was all solved, then he'd know that I was a real supernormal just like him. For once I'd have proven myself.

Three

I guess it's time to admit that my father is a cop. Not a detective or on a SWAT team, just a cop who rides around in a black-and-white cruiser giving people speeding tickets and busting them for creating a disturbance, fighting and stuff like that.

By the time I got home, my dad was putting out the supper. He cooks during the week, and I take over on weekends. Supper is always early from Monday to Friday because he works second shift and has to be at the station by four-thirty. Even though it's about the only time I get to see him except for weekends, sometimes I wish we didn't eat together because the conversation can get pretty tense. Usually it goes something like this:

Dad: We brought in Jimmy McElroy last night, flying higher than a kite. Do you know him?
Me: He's a senior. I've just seen him around school.
Dad: Yeah, well, stay away from him. That kid's only future is behind bars. You don't need friends like that.
Me: He's not my friend!
Dad: He'd better not be.

The worst times are when he's arrested a drunk driver the night before. My mom was killed by a hit-and-run drunk when I was twelve, and getting all drunks off the road is kind of a personal crusade for my father. Maybe he thinks he should have caught that guy before he hit Mom, and he's trying to make up for it.

"We caught that bum Johnny Parks weaving all over Main Street," he'll begin as I shrink down in my chair. "He smelled like a brewery, almost broke the Breathalyzer. Do you know him?"

"No," I answer, trying to make my face an expressionless mask.

"He was coming home from a party at Tony Fasio's. Do you know him?"

"I've seen him around school," I admit.

"You know that if I ever catch you drunk behind the wheel of a car, I'll break your arm."

I say nothing. There's not much chance of it happening. Even though I have a driver's license, he never leaves the car home at night, and I almost have to file an airline flight plan to take it down to the corner on a Saturday.

"Do you hear me?" he shouts, loud enough for the neighbors to hear.

I get up and empty my dinner into the garbage. "Yeah, I hear you," I say, going into the other room.

Before he leaves for work, he always finds me, wherever I am, and messes my hair. I guess it's his way of showing that everything is all right. Maybe a pat on the head makes it all right for him, but it doesn't do anything for me.

Today as we sat over our frozen potpies, I was trying to figure out how to get answers from a demented questioner. My idea was to let him start the questioning, and then I would subtly bring the conversation around to Cathy's disappearance.

"How was school?" he asked. This was always his opening question.

"Okay. The teacher changed my seat in English," I volunteered.

"Why?"

"I don't know," I lied, "but she put me in Cathy McKenna's old seat. I guess she thought the empty desk was depressing the class."

"She should leave it empty to warn you kids what can happen when you aren't careful."

"What do you think happened to her?" I asked, bending over my food and trying to make my words sound casual.

"Last I heard, the detectives in charge of the case decided that she was probably picked up hitchhiking, killed and dumped in the woods somewhere. Maybe the body will turn up later in the spring after all the snow's melted."

The easy way he talked about murder made me sick. I really think he enjoyed putting it as brutally as possible just to see if I would flinch or my hands would shake. Making Cathy sound like a bag of garbage dumped off at the side of the road was his way of testing to see if I was a real man.

"Did you know her?" he asked, more curious than sympathetic.

Automatically I answered, "Not really, I just saw her in class sometimes."

"She must have been kind of wild," he said, wiping the gravy off his plate with a piece of bread.

Why not shut up about her if she's dead! I wanted to scream. Instead I said, "I don't know."

"Good. A girl like that will bring you nothing but trouble."

After he left for the station, I put on a sweatshirt and went out to the garage to shoot some baskets until the knots in my stomach loosened.

It was crazy. On the one hand, he wouldn't let me do much of anything, and the little that he'd let me do he wanted a daily report on. On the other hand, he wanted me to be some kind of tough guy who can take care of himself. Well, how tough can you be when your average day would bore a ten-year-old? Like I said, it was crazy.

To get my mind off my own problems, I decided to review all the facts I had on Cathy's disappearance. It didn't take long. I knew that the police thought Cathy had been kidnapped and maybe murdered by someone who had picked her up hitchhiking. I knew that Jessie didn't think Cathy would hitchhike with a stranger, and I knew that somebody may have erased his name from Cathy's hearts.

Somehow I knew that this wasn't going to be easy. I obviously needed more information because there was no way just to stand there and reason it out. That's one of the things I liked about algebra: if you understood the rules and thought about the problem long enough, you could usually figure it out. You didn't have to go creeping down some dark alley looking for A's, B's and C's.

Finding out how Cathy disappeared was going to be more like science. I would have to get the facts, come up with a theory and test it.

I thought about how nice it would be to talk to Jessie. I could always use the excuse that I wanted more information.

I went inside and got her number off my book. As I dialed, I put my feet up on the table just the way Marlowe would on his old battered desk.

"Hello," a female voice answered.

"Hello, may I speak to Jessie, please?" I asked, using my deep, mature voice.

"This is Jessie. Who's this?"

"This is Lou Dunlop. I need some more information."

"Do you have a cold, Lou? Your voice sounds funny."

"No," I answered in my normal voice. "Well, actually, I may have a little bit of one, but it's nothing serious."

"That's good. What would you like to know? I have the list just about finished, but it isn't very long."

"That's okay, I'll look at it tomorrow. What I was wondering is, exactly when did Cathy disappear? I don't read newspapers much," I concluded weakly.

"Well, there isn't much to know. She left school on November seventeenth, and some people saw her standing in front of the building, but nobody ever saw her again after that. At least, nobody who's telling."

"Okay, thanks."

"Is that all? Do you have any new ideas?"

I couldn't very well say that I just wanted to hear her voice. "There are lots of possibilities. I'm just going to let them all sit in my mind overnight, and maybe I'll have something in the morning." That line didn't seem very convincing, even to me.

"That sounds more like a way to make spaghetti sauce than to solve a crime," she said and hung up.

I sat there listening to the dial tone and heard Marlowe's voice in the back of my mind. "We all have nights like this, kid. It's part of the job."

I just hoped he was right.

Four

I raced out of my first-period history class right at the bell in order to beat everyone else to the home ec room. The teacher, Mrs. Draghetti, was standing in the hall exchanging recipes with the music teacher, so as soon as I got inside the room, I rushed over to examine the table where Cathy used to sit.

There was nothing to see. A few smudged areas might have been hearts, but it was impossible to be sure. On impulse I got down on my hands and knees. It seemed pretty unlikely that there would be much worth seeing under the table, and at first I didn't notice anything except for chewing gum. There was loads of that under there, all different colors squished into different designs. Then I spotted it, scratched in the gray paint on one of the metal side supports, a heart with the words Cathy and Mike written inside it.

"Are you planning to wash the floor?" a voice asked above me.

I jumped and banged my head on the edge of the table. Rubbing the bump that was already starting to form, I looked up and saw Mike Reynolds standing over me.

"No," I answered, trying to come up with a plausible excuse and at the same time wondering if this was *the* Mike. "I just dropped my pen, and it rolled under the table." I pulled the pen out of my pocket to show him, and it sailed out of my hand and across the room.

Mike chuckled. "Good hands there, Lou."

I blushed and went over to pick it up.

"Speaking of good hands, are you going to try out for the baseball team again this year?" he asked. "With Jenkins gone you might get a lot of playing time at first this season."

I'd made the team last year, but tenth graders never got much chance to play. Plus the coach had decided that I was best at first base because of my height, which put me behind Big Bill Jenkins, the team star. Mike was right. With Bill graduated and playing in the minors out in the sticks somewhere, I could get a lot of playing time. But Eric and I had pretty much agreed that only suckers and dumb jocks put out all that effort to make a coach or the school look good. What did the school or coach ever do for you?

"I don't know," I said. "Maybe I will."

"Sign-ups are this week. If you go today, you could come over and shoot baskets with Bill, Frank and me. Once in a while we even get enough guys to play a half-court game."

"Yeah, that would be good, but I'll have to see. I'm kind of busy."

"I guess you hang out a lot with Eric Hannah these days?"

"I see him sometimes. We walk home together."

"Yeah, we're in the same gym class. He's real good at basketball. Bring him along, too, if you come."

"Okay," I said. Probably Eric was really the one they wanted. I didn't care. I knew he wouldn't come, even if I told him.

I watched Mike as he went over to his seat. I tried to remember whether I'd seen him and Cathy talking together a lot. He was kind of dark and skinny.

And although I'd never noticed it before, with his two big front teeth he looked a little bit like a rat or some kind of weasel. Can you tell just by looking at someone whether they're a killer or not? He did shove under the basket a lot, but somehow that wasn't exactly the same thing as being a murderer. Also, he was vice president of the junior class and had a lot of friends; but then, murderers probably have friends, too. I was still wondering what kind of friends murderers have when Mrs. Draghetti began explaining the mysteries of making corn bread.

After English, Jessie and I got together in our usual corner across from the clinic. Because it was Friday, business was slow, and only Psychosomatic Sally was in there, stamping passes for the nurse.

Jessie shoved a small piece of paper into my hand. She was wearing her denim jacket and jeans again, but instead of a work shirt she had on a black T-shirt with Hands Off written on the front in silver sequins. Obviously, one of her more subdued days.

"These are all the places that I could remember Cathy mentioning," she explained.

I looked at the list: the library, Danny's Sweet Shop, Joe's Exxon and the Burger Shack. Just the sorts of places where you would expect to meet assorted criminal types. They get a tough crowd at the library, especially on story-hour day.

I guess my disappointment showed because Jessie said, "It's the best I could do. Those are all the places she ever mentioned. Cathy was kind of odd, you know. She lived in a world of her own."

"Okay," I said with a sigh. "Do you know what she did at these places? For example, what did she do at the library?"

"She read. What would you expect?"

"What did she read?" I asked patiently.

"Oh, all sorts of things, but mostly fiction and a lot of romances. You know," Jessie said with a smile, "*How I Found My Dream Man and We Lived Happily Ever After*, that sort of stuff."

"Did she meet anyone there?"

"I don't know, but I think she was always hoping that some fabulous guy would come along."

"Some guy in shining armor with his horse parked outside who just stopped in to return some overdue books on chivalry."

Jessie gave me a disapproving glance. "Maybe. She liked to dream. Is there anything wrong with that?"

I couldn't think of a quick comeback to that one, so I went on. "What about Danny's?"

"She used to stop there on the way to school to get a cup of coffee or a candy bar. I checked there myself. Danny is sort of a friend of mine, but he didn't know anything."

"What did she stop at Joe's Exxon for—a lube job?"

"I don't know, but once I told her that my car was acting funny, and she said that the mechanic at Joe's was good. I got the idea that he might be a friend of hers."

"Isn't Joe's Exxon the one right up the street from here?"

Jessie nodded.

"Do you know the mechanic's name?"

"No, but what difference would that make?"

Trying to sound casual, I explained about the heart under the table, leaving out the part about banging my head and throwing my pen around.

Her eyes widened. "Do you really think Mike Reynolds did it? I would never have thought he was the type."

"What type is the type?" I asked, trying to sound like a real detective.

"You know," Jessie muttered impatiently, "the weird-looking little guy in the dirty raincoat who gives candy to little girls."

"Cathy was no little girl, and if it was somebody she was going out with, then it stands to reason that he wasn't some old pervert."

"I know," Jessie said, running her fingers through her almost platinum hair, "but I guess I never thought it would be somebody normal. Mike's a real popular guy. If we ask too many questions, we could get into a lot of trouble. Maybe we should take what we know to the police."

I should have been relieved, but instead I got angry. I guess it was because she had gotten me started on this, and now, after I had finally found enough courage to go ahead with it, she wanted to back out.

"We don't *know* anything. We don't have proof that Mike Reynolds did it. There must be thirty Mikes in the school, and it could just as easily be any one of them. If you want to quit, that's fine, but remember, Cathy was your friend, not mine." I took a deep breath.

Jessie leaned back against the wall as if she had been pushed and gave me a long look.

"Wow, I must have hit the wrong button that time," she said, tilting her head back as though she were taking a new look at me.

I grunted eloquently. It seemed the best way to keep the upper hand.

"If we can't be sure whether Mike Reynolds had anything to do with this, what should we do next?" she asked, moving away from the wall and closer to me.

"Follow up our leads. One of us should go to Joe's Exxon, and the other can check out the Burger Shack."

"Julie Simpson works at the Burger Shack. I can get information from her. So maybe you should go to the gas station. You can always give some story about needing work done on your car."

If I had a car, I thought, but I didn't want to bring that up. Maybe they could oil my shoes. Anyway, I agreed.

Just before we separated, Jessie touched my arm. "Are you really sure you want to keep on with this?" she asked, seeming concerned about me this time.

Of course not. I want to go home, have some cookies and milk and hide under the bed, a gutless little coward in my mind screamed. But I stayed calm. "Hey," I said with a careless shrug, "a good detective tracks down every lead, no matter where it goes."

Somewhere in the back of my mind, Marlowe chuckled.

Five

Have you ever noticed how places start to look different when you go there to do something that you really don't want to do? Take, for example, the supermarket you've been in at least once every week of your life—it looks and even smells different the day you walk in to ask for a job. Or the high school you've been going by since you were a little kid—it really is bigger and scarier when you show up for the first day of school.

That's the way it was with Joe's Exxon. I'd walked by it every day for years, and it always looked like any one of thirty stations in town: a re-

volving sign in front, a rack of oil cans, six pumps
and two garages next to a sleazy office. But today
what I saw was how far back it was from the road,
that there was a vacant lot filled with low-hanging
trees on one side and how you couldn't see into the
garage through the dirty windows. Also, it's amazing how a place that's usually swarming with people can sometimes be so empty. To me, it looked
like the loneliest place in the world.

I hunched over a little, tried to ignore my heart
thumping and walked into the office. Going from
the sunlight into the dark room blinded me, and it
was a couple of seconds before I realized that
someone was working under the hood of a car in
the garage nearest the office. I took a few steps out
into the garage and accidentally kicked some kind
of metal tool that was lying on the ground. It made
a noise that wasn't much louder than a firecracker
exploding in a garbage can. The guy bending over
the car engine straightened up. He was my height
but about twice as big—an older kid, maybe nine-
teen or twenty.

"What can I do for you?" he asked. I was surprised that he didn't growl.

"Er, well, I wanted to see about an oil change."
That sounded safe.

"Sure. I didn't hear you drive up."

"Well, I don't exactly have my car with me," I said, feeling stupider by the minute.

"It's going to be kind of hard to change the oil, then," he said with a grin that made him look almost human.

"Yeah, well, I'm a friend, er, used to be a friend of Cathy's."

The smile vanished, and he moved toward me from around the car. In his right hand was the largest wrench I'd ever seen.

"I knew that somebody would find out sooner or later," he said sadly, as though he regretted what he had to do.

Have you ever been so scared that your mind kept telling your legs to move but nothing happened? I just stood there as he came toward me. Over the pocket of his shirt was stitched Mike in red thread. I concentrated on that.

When he was about an arm's length away, I finally took a clumsy step backward, slipped in some oil and sat down hard on the concrete floor. I put one arm up to cover my head and vaguely wondered what the sound of metal on bone would be like and whether I would hear it when it came.

Instead, what I heard was the sound of metal on concrete as the wrench bounced on the floor near my feet. After a couple of long seconds I looked up.

He was standing over me with his hand outstretched.

"C'mon, get up!" I took his hand and got pulled to my feet. "I didn't mean to scare you," he continued unconvincingly.

My knees were wobbling so much that I almost sat right down again. I must have looked pretty bad because he suggested that we sit on some old bucket seats over in the corner, and he got us a couple of sodas from the machine out front.

"I guess I did frighten you, coming over with that wrench and all," he said with a grin that lit up a face that was dark with grease and oil smudges.

I shrugged, which was about the closest I could come to acting cool at the moment.

"But the thing is," he went on, "you surprised me. I didn't think that anyone knew about Cathy and me. She said she didn't tell anyone at school, and the police never came around to ask me any questions after she disappeared."

"Were you two going out together?" I managed to croak. Now that my heart was pumping again, I remembered that I was supposed to be asking questions.

"Not really. At first I just used to see her walking by the station after school. Then one day in late September, when it was still pretty warm, she stopped in for a soda. We talked for a little while, and pretty soon she was stopping by every day on the way home.''

"What did you two do together?''

"It was nothing like that,'' he said, giving me a hostile glance that made me wish I'd kept my mouth shut. "She never stayed long, and all we did was talk. But we had some really good talks.''

"But you never went out?''

"I asked her out just before she disappeared, but she said that she had to settle things with some guy before we could do that.''

"Who?''

"She wouldn't tell me. Said he was really just a friend but that she cared a lot for him because he needed her.''

We sat there drinking our sodas, watching the sun try to shine through the dirty windows.

"How did you find out about me?'' he finally asked, as though it didn't matter much.

I explained about the hearts and how I was trying to find out what had happened.

He listened carefully and thought for a moment. "It's strange that she would do that. She was always careful that people from school wouldn't see her here. When I asked her what difference it made, she said she just believed in keeping her private life private." He sighed. "I always figured she was just ashamed to be seen with an older guy who dropped out of school to pump gas. Anyway, I don't know why she'd write my name on her desk."

He sat there holding the soda bottle and looking down at the oil spots on the floor, as though, if he connected them with lines like a game of dot to dot, it would all make sense.

I stood up and found my legs. They were just about ready to start working again.

"You know what I missed most after I dropped out?" he asked half talking to himself.

I shook my head.

"The other kids. I never saw my friends much after I left. We just didn't have anything to talk about anymore. But that's what Cathy could do. Boy! Could she talk. Not boring stuff but good things, and after a while you'd be talking, too. It was really something."

I started backing out of the garage. "Thanks, Mike. I'm sorry about Cathy. I'll let you know if I find out anything."

He just looked up at me. A couple of tears had streaked the grease on his face. I didn't know what to say, so I turned and hurried out into the sunlight.

I rushed up the street and turned down along the tracks. When we didn't meet right after school for some reason or other, Eric and I would wait at The Clearing for a while to see if the other one showed up. I wanted to tell him about what had just happened, but I kept remembering that this was something I had to do on my own. I was going to prove that he wasn't wrong in having me as a friend. That was one of the things I liked about hanging around with Eric: he made me try to be a little bit better than I really was.

I went into The Clearing and saw him sitting on one of the crates. He was watching his cigarette burn down and looking at the ground, sort of the way Mike had been.

"How's it going, Eric?" I said sitting on the other crate, pretending that it had been a normal afternoon.

"Where were you?" he asked without looking up from the ground.

"I had to go sign up for baseball tryouts. There was a long line, so I had to wait," I said quickly.

"I thought you'd decided not to play this year. Something about the other guys being dumb jocks," he said, flicking his cigarette butt across into the bushes.

"I'm still not sure yet what I'll do. Probably I won't even make the team. I haven't been doing much training lately," I said, taking a cigarette from the pack Eric had next to him on the crate.

He smiled a little. "I got some information from a travel agency on the Virgin Islands," he said, pulling a handful of folders out of his jacket pocket and handing them to me. He was always getting things from different agencies. All he had to do was go in and smile, and they gave him almost anything he wanted. He made a great impression on older people.

Almost the whole winter we'd been talking about how great it would be to live somewhere in the Caribbean. Somewhere warm where there was always a gentle breeze off the ocean and palm trees and all that stuff. A place where I wouldn't have to drag myself off to school and worry about whether I was going to act like a jerk that day.

I looked at the pictures of the islands in the folder and could feel the tightness in my stomach disappear. I could feel the sun on my face and see those funny little lights it makes even when you have your eyes closed. I just wanted things to be perfect: sun, sea, sand and no school the next day. Is that too much to ask? I could almost live on the beach like a seashell and go to sleep to the sound of the waves rolling onto the shore. No decisions, no problems, every day the same and as perfect as the one before.

"What do you think?" asked Eric.

"Looks great," I said, still far away on the beach. Somehow I didn't think anyone would chase me with a wrench once I was there.

"We can leave at the end of June, right after school gets out. The agent told me about cottages right on the beach at St. John that we could rent for a couple of months."

I came back to reality with a bump. In December this had been just talk. You know, thinking about the way we'd like things to be someday. But this was now.

"I don't see how I can plan a vacation when I don't have any money," I said.

"I told you before, my mom is loaded. She'll be happy to pay for both of us, and she'll never miss it."

I had met Mrs. Hannah once at Eric's house. She seemed quiet, almost shy, even though she looked really fashionable, like a middle-aged model. I got the idea that she would do almost anything Eric wanted, and she liked me because I was his only close friend. She probably could send us both around the world and never think twice about it.

Eric told me once that his father was paying alimony through the nose, but since he was some kind of hotshot corporation lawyer, Eric said he could afford it. But the idea of accepting that big a favor from anyone, even from Eric, made me uncomfortable.

"My father will never go along with it," I objected.

"Sure he will. Your dad likes me. I can talk him into it. I'll explain what a great lesson in independence it will be for us and how nothing can happen to you as long as you stick with me," Eric explained confidently.

"Thanks. Maybe I should take along a nurse to push my wheelchair."

"You know what I mean!" Eric's light blue eyes almost glowed with enthusiasm. "I have to make it sound good for your dad, but we'll have a great time."

"Sure, well, I'll have to think about it." Suddenly I just wanted to go home and think some more about Cathy's disappearance. Somehow that seemed more real right now than all this island stuff.

"Yeah, do that," Eric answered coldly. I could tell that he was disappointed because I wasn't more excited; but I knew that, once this case was solved and everybody knew all, he would understand why I had to put first things first.

Six

My father and I had our usual friendly table conversation. Somebody under the age of twenty-five had broken into Johnson's Liquors, and my father was questioning me as if he thought I'd helped carry out fifty cases of Schlitz and a bottle of muscatel. Finally, after ten minutes of his cross-examination, I decided that a guy who faced down maniacs with wrenches didn't have to put up with this kind of crap. So I told him that I couldn't have done it because I only stole Miller's. He looked shocked, and we finished eating in silence.

I really wanted to talk about what had happened that afternoon, but there was only one person I could talk to about it, so after my father left, I gave Jessie a call. She listened without comment to my description of what had happened at the gas station. I changed it around a little so that I didn't sound like quite such a jerk, but the basic information was right.

"Well, that kills that lead" was all she said.

Expecting something more in the way of a compliment on my bravery or, at least, on my persistence, I said stubbornly, "He could still be the one."

"Anything is possible," Jessie said easily, "but he doesn't seem to have much of a motive. And if he was a crazy and did kill her, then why are you still walking around?"

Even though it made sense, that wasn't something I needed to be reminded of.

"What did you find out at the Burger Shack?" I asked, secretly hoping she had been equally unsuccessful.

"I thought you'd never ask! Julie said that two days before Cathy disappeared she had an argument in the Burger Shack with Debbie Hayes. Debbie caught her sitting at a table having a shake with her boyfriend, Rodger."

"Sounds like a soap opera," I remarked.

"Doesn't it? They were talking loudly, and Debbie made Rodger leave with her. Julie said that Cathy looked really upset."

"That sounds like a good lead," I admitted. I figured I'd be big about the whole thing and show that I could give compliments even when I didn't get any.

"There's still more!" Jessie went on quickly. "Julie said she saw Debbie stop and give Cathy a ride from school the day she disappeared."

"Didn't Julie tell the police?"

"I guess she figured they would know, that Debbie or somebody else told them. And remember, the police have been talking as if some weirdo kidnapped her. I guess Julie didn't think it was important, and it was easy to get her to promise not to tell anyone that we were investigating."

"Great, but what do we do now?" I asked.

"Can you meet me at the Burger Shack in half an hour?"

I almost said yes but realized that without a car I could never make it in time.

"No. I'll have to walk, and it will take me more like an hour."

"Okay, I'll pick you up in ten minutes. Be ready to go," she said crisply.

"Do you know where I live?"

"Of course," she replied and hung up.

More surprises. I guess you never know how much other people know about you. You go through school thinking that nobody notices you, but actually nothing stays a secret for very long.

I got ready in a hurry, putting on my best jeans and a blue pullover sweater. I waited by the living room window with the lights off and looked out at the dark street. I tried to decide whether I was more nervous or excited, decided that it was a little bit of both and that it didn't seem so bad. That was good because sometimes I get even more nervous when I worry about being nervous, if that makes any sense.

In exactly nine minutes a Volkswagen Beetle pulled up at the curb, and the driver gave the horn an aggressive little toot.

I ran out and piled into the little car. Jessie sat behind the wheel, smiling.

"Sorry, but I couldn't get the Rolls for tonight. It's in the garage for repairs."

"Please, let's not talk about garages, okay?"

"Yeah. I could tell you were a little shaken up. You never even asked me why I wanted to go to the Burger Shack," she said with a knowing smile.

"For a chocolate shake?" I was hoping this would turn into a first date.

"Very funny. Debbie hangs out there for a while most nights, so I figured that maybe we could talk to her. You'll be safe. I don't think she'll be carrying a wrench around with her," added Jessie with a nasty smile.

"She doesn't need one. Her natural equipment is deadly enough," I said to get even. Although she was a little short, Debbie had a great figure, and she always looked as if she had just stepped out of the pages of a fashion magazine.

Jessie was undisturbed. "Every school has at least one Debbie. She's the one who wears a little too much makeup, puts on a dress when everyone else is wearing jeans, makes eyes at all the male teachers and thinks anyone in pants is hot to get her."

I was glad it was dark in the car because I must have gotten red. That was exactly the way I felt whenever I saw Debbie. To cover up my embarrassment I said, "Yeah, and her fingernails should be registered as weapons."

"Don't worry," said Jessie, swinging the car into the parking lot. "If she tries to gouge your eyes out, I'll deck her with my bag. It's heavy enough."

That made me feel kind of small, so I didn't say any more.

We walked into the Burger Shack and looked around for Debbie. "Great decor," Marlowe whispered in my mind, "the finest in high quality plastic." I shrugged. What did he expect, mahogany and broadloom carpets? Jessie was looking at me oddly.

"Are you okay?" she asked. "I can do this alone if you're not feeling well."

"I'm fine. I was just checking out the scene," I said confidently.

Continuing to look doubtful, Jessie pointed to a corner where Debbie sat talking to a girl I didn't recognize.

We went over to their table, with Jessie leading the way, and said hello.

Debbie gave us a puzzled expression, probably wondering why we were bothering her. Jessie didn't leave her in doubt for long.

"We'd like to talk to you about something at school," she said, glaring at the other girl, "and we'd like to talk to you alone."

The other girl looked surprised, and Debbie's face got a sort of tight, angry look. So I turned to the girl and said quietly, "Could you excuse us for a minute? We have some questions about history that we'd like to ask Debbie."

The girl glanced at Debbie, then she slid out of the booth and walked over to a group of kids standing near the door.

"What's this all about?" Debbie asked as Jessie sat down across from her and I moved in next to her. She played nervously with the straw in her shake. There were dark red lipstick stains on the end.

"We just want to ask you a few questions," I said, giving her my best smile. If she wasn't a murderess, I still might want to go out with her sometime.

"About what?"

Before I could gradually work around to the topic, Jessie interrupted, "We know you picked Cathy up outside school the last day she was seen. We want to know what happened to her." Good old Jessie, full of tact, as usual.

Debbie tried to slide out of the booth, which was hard because I didn't move and she couldn't very well climb over me. Her face was twisted almost into a snarl, and she didn't look very pretty anymore. When I didn't move, she started to raise her hand with its long crimson fingernails. I jerked my head back, but before she could move, Jessie's hand shot out and pinned her arm to the table.

"Don't be a fool, Debbie," she whispered. "You can either talk to us or go to the police."

Debbie sat there looking sullen.

"Look, we don't want to go to the cops or get you in trouble. We know you didn't do anything wrong," I said soothingly. "We just want to know what happened." I thought about patting her hand but decided against it.

Debbie hesitated, then nodded, and Jessie released her arm.

"There's really nothing to tell," she said in a tired voice. "I picked Cathy up out in front of school and gave her a ride for a few blocks. That's all."

"Where did you let her off?" I asked.

"Up the street from the school, across from the Exxon station," she replied.

"You weren't exactly friends. Why did you give her a ride?" asked Jessie.

Debbie looked as if she wanted to tell Jessie to stuff it, but all she said was, "I just wanted to warn her to stay away from Rodger."

"What exactly did you two talk about, Debbie?" I asked before Jessie could say any more.

"Cathy didn't get a chance to say much because I was really mad at her for talking to Rodger here that night, you know."

I nodded.

"But I know now that it wasn't her fault. In fact," she paused and sighed, "I've known for a long time that it isn't other girls who chase Rodger, it's Rodger who chases them."

More softly Jessie asked, "Did she say anything, Debbie, anything at all?"

Debbie wrinkled her brow and looked thoughtful. It wasn't an expression that came naturally to her, but if she wasn't a genius, she did look pretty good in her white sweater and jeans.

"Just as she was getting out of the car, after listening to me rant and rave, she gave me a sweet smile and said, 'I'm not interested in Rodger. I've already got somebody who means more to me than Rodger will ever mean to you.'"

"And you let her out right across from the Exxon station?" I asked.

"Just a little past it. I had to stop for a train going through, and she hopped out there."

"Did you see where she went?" asked Jessie.

"No, I just put my foot on the gas and went. How was I supposed to know she would disappear?" Debbie demanded as though we had accused her of something.

Neither one of us said anything, and Debbie stared out the window at the traffic. Then she said,

"You don't know how often since then I've wished that I had just taken her home."

We slid out of the booth. Jessie asked me to wait for a minute while she said a few words to Julie, who was behind the counter wearing her best Burger Shack smile and dressed to look like a barbershop pole.

As I stood by the door, Rodger swaggered in and brushed past me. He strolled over to Debbie's table and sat down as if he were doing her a big favor. He was the kind of guy girls would probably say was good-looking: dark, wavy hair, brown eyes and an athletic build, although he was a little on the short side. The thing was, though, he always had this smirk on his face. You know what I mean, he looked at you as if you had just done something stupid and he was going to tell everyone about it.

Jessie finished talking to Julie, and we walked out into the parking lot.

"Hey! You two, hold it!" a voice shouted.

We turned around. I already knew it was going to be Rodger. He walked up to us, and in the parking lot light I could see the usual smirk firmly in place.

"I don't know what you two think you're up to," he began, then he looked at me. "Especially you. I think you should stay out of this, or you might get hurt. I don't think you'd like that."

I wasn't really afraid, which surprised even me. I was about a head taller, and anyone who looked in the mirror as much as Rodger did probably wasn't much of a fighter. Plus I was on a case, and you had to expect some of this. But the thing is, I never know what to say when someone starts insulting me in a serious way. I'd feel like a jerk standing there saying "You, too" or "Your mother wears boxer shorts," but I'd also feel like a jerk just standing there not answering. The only alternative was to break his face, but that would give him an excuse to break mine. Problems, always problems.

Fortunately, Jessie filled in the gap.

"Get lost, pretty boy," she said with a smirk that outdid even Rodger's. "Go back in the john and comb your hair again."

Maybe she figured Rodger wouldn't try to break *her* face or that I would protect her. I wasn't too sure about either one.

Rodger looked stunned. His smirk slipped, and his eyes opened wide. Probably he wasn't used to girls talking to him like that, and he certainly wasn't used to Jessie.

"Look, I'm just going to say this once. Leave Debbie alone! She doesn't know anything about what happened to Cathy."

"And how much do you know?" Jessie shot back.

For a second I thought he really was going to slug her, and I got ready to make a grab for his arm.

"Rodger, come back inside. I'm getting lonely," Debbie whined from the door of the Burger Shack.

"In a minute," he snapped. "Just stay out of my way, you two, or else you'll be in a world of trouble," he said and swaggered back into the building.

As Jessie and I walked over to her car, I took her hand. It probably surprised her as much as it did me, but I felt just then as if I needed a friend. I even suggested that we go back to my house and discuss things over a cup of coffee and a doughnut. This time I don't think Jessie was as surprised as I was.

Seven

We sat in the living room with mugs of coffee and tried to keep the powdered sugar on the doughnuts and off our clothes and the furniture. Neither of us had said much since the scene in the parking lot.

Finally Jessie licked the sugar off her fingers and said, "I don't think we're any nearer an answer than when we started. We don't know who Mike is. If he's the guy in the garage, it doesn't make sense that she would scratch his name on her desk when she was trying to keep their friendship a secret. And you said that the guy did seem to care about Cathy."

"He could just have been a good actor," I said. This kind of work could turn you into a cynic fast.

Jessie nodded. "And we don't know whether Debbie was telling us the truth, and even if she was, we still don't know where Cathy was going."

"Don't forget Mike Reynolds. His name on the desk in the home ec room is quite a coincidence," I said.

"Somehow I just can't see him doing it. You know, his father is president of Consolidated Chemical."

"Even rich people commit crimes," I said. I'd heard that from my father often enough.

"I suppose."

We both gave deep sighs at the same time and then laughed. In the yellow glow of the lamp, Jessie looked different. She looked softer somehow; her aggressive, chip-on-the-shoulder attitude had disappeared. She leaned forward to sip her coffee, and a necklace swung out from inside her shirt.

"What's that?" I asked, pointing at a silver charm hanging on the chain.

She held it up, and I could see that it was a question mark.

"What does that mean?"

She gave me a long look, like she was wondering whether to give me a simple, snappy answer or get serious and tell me the truth.

"I wear it because I think everybody who's really alive is looking for the answer to some big question," she said cautiously, as though waiting to see if I was going to laugh. I didn't.

"Do you know what I mean?" she asked.

I nodded, but I wasn't sure that I did understand.

"So what question are you looking for an answer to?" she asked quickly.

"Why should I go on living?" I blurted out before I even knew what I was saying. If she was surprised or shocked, it didn't show. She just looked thoughtful.

I took a moment to get myself together, then asked, "What about you? You must have a question."

"Maybe mine is a little like yours. I want to know when we begin to live."

"How do you mean?"

"You know, when is life going to start? Teachers, parents and everybody, they always say that someday you'll be able to do what you want to do but not now. Right now you have to do what they say, and that's really boring. I've been around seventeen years, and sometimes I feel that nothing has really happened to me. I'm tired of getting ready to live. I want to start living.''

I looked down at my coffee. She had said it all so fast and seemed so angry that I didn't know what to say.

''I see what you mean,'' I began, ''but aren't they right in a way? We do have the rest of our lives to do all sorts of things.''

''Yeah, but do you see adults enjoying themselves, doing all those things they couldn't do when they were kids? No! They forget all that stuff and start making money, having a family. If you don't do it when you're young, then you never will,'' Jessie concluded, twisting the necklace in her fingers.

''But when you're older, it's easier to handle things,'' I argued. ''There are a lot of things you're not ready for when you're a kid. Things that can get you all messed up.''

''Sure, it's easier then because they've already got you conditioned. You're programmed, so you don't even *want* to do crazy things anymore. They won't let you start living until you're just like them.''

I shrugged. I didn't want to get into a fight with her, plus I was thinking how maybe she did have a point.

"It's just like my brother, Vic," she went on. "He's a smart guy. He did really well in high school, and my parents loved it. Now he's in college, getting good grades, but he's got an ulcer the size of a quarter. They've already had him in the hospital twice when it started bleeding. My parents get upset and everything, but what they really care about is whether he keeps getting good grades so that he can become a doctor, just like my father."

What she had said got me to tell her a little about my father being a cop and the way he never let me do much.

She nodded her head enthusiastically. "You can't let parents think they can run your life. You've got to show them that you're a person, too."

"Is that why you dress so funny?" I asked a little nervously. "Is it just to freak out your parents?"

I was relieved when she smiled. "Partly, I guess. They get disgusted with the way I dress. When my father is mad at me, he says I look like a tramp. But I don't do it just to upset them. I like these clothes. They're not phony. They let people know what I'm like, and I'm comfortable in them."

"I don't want this to come as a surprise or anything, but you let people know what you're like pretty fast by the things you say. Rodger won't be the same, at least not until tomorrow."

"Yeah, it was great seeing the expression on his face, the creep. But I'm glad you were there; he looked pretty mean."

"Do you think he's mean enough to have killed Cathy if she told him to get lost?" I asked, feeling good that she thought of me as protection.

"He's such a conceited weasel, I wouldn't think it would matter enough to him. But who knows?"

We didn't know much of anything, so we sort of slumped down in our chairs and studied the carpet. I was tempted to forget the whole thing and just ask Jessie to go out with me on normal dates. But I wasn't sure that she would. I figured that probably this Cathy business was her only reason for being willing to go out with me at all.

Finally she said, "Well, we haven't checked out the library yet. Maybe there are some leads there."

"Oh, yeah, that's a real den of thieves."

"Do you have a better idea?"

She had me there, so I said politely, "Well, it's a long shot, but it's worth a try, I suppose."

Jessie nodded. "It's getting late," she said, standing and slowly stretching. Her shirt pulled tight over her body, and suddenly, finding out what had happened to Cathy seemed less important.

"It's time for me to go. Thanks for the coffee and doughnut. Maybe we can get to the library tomorrow night."

I walked her to the front door, and she stood on the top step for a long time as though waiting for me to do something. Then she just sighed and said good night. I watched her car pull away from the curb and felt that somehow I had missed something.

Again Marlowe nagged at the back of my mind, "For a bright kid, you can be pretty stupid sometimes."

Eight

Have you ever had one of those days when your head feels like a toxic-waste site? I had lain awake for a long time after I'd gone to bed the night before, thinking about Jessie, Debbie and Rodger. Then my father had come in and tried to get ready for bed without making a lot of noise, which just made it seem louder. Finally, when I was sure that I would never sleep again, I dropped off. Sometimes things happen that way.

I had Algebra first period, and it was probably my best subject. But today, whenever Mr. Caruthers looked in my direction, I sort of scrunched down in the seat and didn't look him in the eye. There hadn't been time to do the homework, and I wasn't feeling very sharp.

In English Jessie gave me a smile as she walked in right after the bell. Mrs. Kasterson was still going on about the Transcendentalists and was talking about some essay called "Self-Reliance" by this guy Ralph Waldo Emerson. He was like Thoreau, who was big on how everyone should march to the sound of his own drummer, and stuff like that. That's easy to say when you're a big-shot writer who doesn't have to work for a living, but it's hard when you're a kid and can't even go to the bathroom without a pass. But I could tell by the look on her face that Jessie was eating this stuff up.

At the end of class, she quickly whispered to me that she'd call me after supper and went off without another word. I drifted through the rest of my classes. A really wasted day. I probably wouldn't remember anything about it tomorrow.

I left the building after my last class and cut across to the gym. I figured that I'd better sign up for baseball since I'd told Eric I'd done it yesterday. But there was a crowd of kids standing around the main door staring at an ambulance, so I wandered over to see what was happening. The front doors swung open as the school nurse and one of the ambulance attendants came rushing out with someone in a wheelchair. As they rolled him by, I recognized Mike Roeper. "Is everyone in this school named Mike?" Marlowe whispered in my mind.

Roeper was leaning way forward in the chair, and they had him strapped in so that he wouldn't fall out. As he went by, he looked at us but didn't really seem to see anyone. Suddenly he shouted, "I'll pay fifty dollars for those wheel covers! I'll pay it!"

A couple of the kids standing around applauded, and a few laughed in a nervous sort of way. Somebody said, "Yeah, we'll get you those wheel covers, Mike." Mike gave a big, stupid smile and waved, but he didn't know what the heck was going on. In a few seconds they had him out of the chair, onto a stretcher and into the ambulance. I watched as it pulled away from the curb and nosed out through the line of yellow school buses.

"Must have mixed some things together, or else he's on some pretty strange stuff," said someone standing next to me.

I turned and saw Marty Stanton. He's a cop and was my father's partner until last year when they assigned him to the school patrol. That got started when the board of education received complaints from a lot of parents about vandalism and the use of drugs in the junior and senior high schools. The board decided that putting a uniformed cop in school would prove that they were taking the complaints seriously. Marty got the job because he was in his twenties, kind of cool and knew how to speak to kids. Actually, he was a pretty good guy and would always stop to talk to me if he wasn't busy.

"Yeah," I agreed, "Mike seemed to be really out of it."

"The whole time they were wheeling him down the hall from the clinic, all he kept talking about were those darned wheel covers," said Marty. "It would almost be funny if it weren't so sad. Another joke is that the board of education has this new policy that they're going to press charges in every case of drug use on school property."

I told him that the principal had been announcing it over the intercom every day for the past month, until by now the whole class would laugh when he began, "This is the final warning..." for the thirtieth time.

Marty motioned me away from the crowd of kids still standing around the spot where Mike had been loaded into the ambulance, and we went and leaned on the side of his cruiser.

"Just between you and me, the charges will probably never get anywhere. A lot of folks in this town have got money, so when one of their kids gets in trouble, they'll come to the school, have a cozy chat with the principal, and little Jennifer or Jason will get off with a couple of days' suspension. It's a waste of my time being here."

"Then why push for the strict rules in the first place?" I asked.

"Because every parent is sure it's somebody else's kid who's trashing the building or getting stoned in the bathrooms. It's always easier to send somebody else's kid to jail."

"Maybe there shouldn't be any law against using drugs in the first place," I ventured. I felt pretty sure I could say that to Marty. My father was another story. He'd have me up on charges for even suggesting such an un-American idea.

"Yeah, well, we could argue about legalizing pot all day, but Mike was into more than a couple of joints in the boys' room. When they have to wheel you out of the school building babbling about wheel covers, it's time to find a different habit." Marty shook his head. "Mike just doesn't act like a guy with plans for the future."

"How do you mean?"

"I've talked to him a few times. He's tired of life here and gets a rest by letting his mind take a trip. Probably being able to do that is the only thing that keeps him going." Marty paused and rubbed his face with both hands. "We all feel that way sometimes. This happens to be Mike's personal method of dealing with it."

"But Cathy wasn't like that, was she?" I asked on a sudden inspiration. My father always claimed that abrupt changes of subject often got a suspect to tell you more than he wanted to, and Marty had probably been the first cop to investigate Cathy's disappearance.

Unfortunately, Marty seemed wise to my move and gave me a sharp, almost hostile, glance. "Of course she wasn't. Why do you bring her up?"

"Because a lot of people seem to think she suddenly decided that school bored her and took off with the first person who offered her a free ride out of town. But I didn't think she was like that."

"Did you know her well?" Marty asked, trying to make it sound casual, but I knew this had gone from being a friendly conversation to an interrogation.

Questions, with cops it's always questions, but I remembered that to get information you had to give some. The trick was to give less than you got.

"Only a little," I answered carefully. "My English teacher moved me to Cathy's old seat the other day, so I was thinking about her."

Marty was silent for a moment, turning over my story in his mind. At last I guess he accepted it because he said, "I only talked to her a few times, but I'd agree with you, she seemed pretty happy."

"Did you investigate her disappearance?"

"Yeah, I spoke to some of her friends, searched her locker, things like that. But there was nothing unusual. She was a nice kid, maybe a little less mature than some, who kept to herself a lot but not enough for anyone to think she was strange."

"What about her parents? Did you question them?"

"I didn't, but the two detectives assigned to the case did. They have no idea what could have happened to her. Both of them work, and as long as Cathy was home for supper by six, didn't complain and was doing okay at school, they weren't concerned." Marty held out a hand as though asking my opinion. "Hell, why should they be? She only went out at night to go to the library. It wasn't like she was wild or anything. They figured that there was no reason to worry."

We both studied the sidewalk for a while. "I have to go to the hospital and get the doctor's word on what's in Roeper's system for my report," he said finally, opening the door of the cruiser.

"So you go along with the idea that somebody got her into a car and kidnapped her?"

"That's what we always say when a kid disappears and we don't know how or why. But that doesn't make it any less possible that it's the truth. Probably it's as good a guess as any, although I know that's not very satisfying."

He got in the car and offered me a lift part of the way home. I shook my head. "Then this is where it ends? You just give up?"

"Lou, thousands of kids disappear every year. Some of them even from fancy towns like this. And only a small percentage are ever found. What can I say?"

I nodded, and with a wave he headed out in the same direction as the ambulance.

I walked over to the gym, signed up for the team and got the permission slip for my father to sign. Mike Reynolds and a few other guys were shooting baskets, and they called for me to come over. But I shook my head and went back outside. Cathy had wanted to live, and it seemed that someone hadn't let her. People sure don't always get what they want or maybe even what they deserve. There were so many things going through my mind that I didn't even want to see Eric, so I took the long route home.

Nine

Jessie's car pulled up to the curb, and I hopped in. Tonight she was wearing a sweatshirt over a turtleneck with the usual jeans and boots. The sweatshirt had Fragile: Handle With Care stenciled on the front in the same kind of printing that they put on shipping cartons. I wasn't sure what to make of that, but it had to be an improvement over Hands Off.

"Are you all set, Sherlock?" she asked as we perked along down the street.

"Yeah, but I still don't know how we're going to find out anything at the library."

"Easy, we just ask Naomi," answered Jessie, as though I should have known all along.

"Who's she?"

"She works there."

"Why should she tell us anything?"

"She's sort of a friend of mine."

Well, I hope she's more talkative than you are, I thought. "Maybe she doesn't know anything," I ventured aloud.

"She does. She already told me that Cathy used to talk to Michael Schuman a lot. He works there, too."

"Another Mike," I groaned. "Did everyone name their male offspring Michael seventeen years ago?"

"Not quite, and he's definitely a Michael and not a Mike. But you must know him. He's that skinny, dark-haired kid who always wears a suit to school and plays chess all the time."

I did vaguely remember him from gym class in junior high. He was always one of the last guys picked for teams, which bothers some kids a lot, but Schuman always acted as if it didn't mean a thing. Even when he was playing some sport badly, which was usually the case, he looked like he was thinking of something else. Maybe he was making chess moves in his head.

"He's not going to be easy to question," I said.

"Why not?"

"I don't know, but he's not on the same wavelength with everybody else."

"Don't worry, a few tough questions will get him on the same signal. Just leave it to me," she said with her usual incredible confidence.

The library is a large stone building that was built seventy or eighty years ago and looks it. When you walk in, that sort of musty smell of old books and floor wax hits you right away. It also has this very high ceiling, and I bet with all that stone you could get a great echo if you yelled. Of course all the librarians would probably have heart failure. Just my luck, they would charge me with a felony—screaming with intent to kill.

Naomi was shelving books on the second floor when we finally tracked her down. She was small and kind of cute with dark hair and large brown eyes. I was surprised she would work there hidden away behind all those books, with only librarians to talk to. But Jessie had told me that she wanted to be a librarian someday herself, so I guess she figured it was good practice.

After the introductions had been made, Jessie asked, "We'd like to talk to Schuman. Do you know where he's working tonight?"

"Where he always works," Naomi answered, trying to reach a top shelf with a book. I gave her a hand, and she smiled gratefully. Jessie shot me a contemptuous glance. "He's always in the basement. That's where they keep the periodicals and the overflow of books that we can't fit on the shelves."

"What does he do down there?" I asked.

"Well, let's say you want a book that isn't on the shelf. First, you go to the main desk and the librarian checks the card to make sure the book hasn't been taken out. If it's there and not on the shelf, she calls down to Michael, and he sends it up on a dumbwaiter."

"A dumbwaiter?" asked Jessie.

"Yeah, you know, one of those little elevators that you can put things on to send them up or down," Naomi explained.

"How do we get to see this guy if he never comes upstairs?" I asked.

"Your best bet is to ask for the key to the rest room. The rest rooms are downstairs, and there's a door marked Employees Only. It's never locked, so go in there and you'll find Michael."

"Is that where Cathy used to meet him?" Jessie asked.

"That's right. She'd spend around half an hour down there with him a couple of afternoons a week. Then she would come up to the main floor and read for a while until around four-thirty."

"Where did she go from here?" asked Jessie.

"I don't know. I think that sometimes she went home and other times stopped off at the Burger Shack."

"Thanks, Naomi. Let's go see what this guy has to say, Lou. You go get the key to the men's room, and I'll get the key to the ladies' room a minute or two later. No sense making the librarian suspicious," said Jessie.

I got the key at the desk. It was attached to a huge block of wood. Were they afraid someone would steal it?

I met up with Jessie in the downstairs hall.

"Well, let's do it," she muttered, walking right up to the Employees Only door and pushing it open wide. I hurried to keep up with her.

We went through the door, and the world went black. Well, not black exactly, but pretty dark. Shelves of books towered over us on either side. The only light was at the end of the long aisle where someone was bent over a desk.

Jessie marched down the aisle with me right behind. You'd have thought that the sound of her boots on the stone floor would have made whoever it was look up, but the figure didn't move. She was making enough noise to wake the dead, I thought, and went a little cold at the idea.

He was slumped over the desk, facedown on a book that said "Chess Moves for Champions" across the top of the page. He didn't move. Before I could stop her, Jessie reached forward and touched him on the shoulder. I knew you weren't supposed to move bodies before the police got there.

His head turned and his eyes *opened*. Then the eyes blinked, and the head came up off the table. The hair on the back of my neck must have been standing straight up, and even Jessie pulled her hand back as if it had been burned. His hand reached out for a pair of black plastic-framed glasses next to the book, and he shoved them on his face. He stared at us and blinked again. It was Schuman, all right.

"Sorry, I must have been asleep," he mumbled. Then he took a second look at us, especially at Jessie, peering like an owl through his thick glasses. "Who are you?"

"I'm Jessie Phillips, and this is Lou Dunlop. We're friends of Cathy's, and we want to ask you a few questions about her."

That woke him up, and he got a stubborn look on his face.

"You're not supposed to be in here. This is for employees only."

"Yeah, yeah, so answer a few questions and we'll leave," said Jessie, sitting on the edge of his desk.

He looked at her rear end as if it were contaminating his desk and got even more stubborn. "Unless you leave, I'll call upstairs and have the librarians get the police," he said, pushing his glasses further up on his nose and pointing to the phone on his desk.

With my luck my father would show up and take me away in handcuffs.

"You're a friend of Cathy's," I said in my most reasonable tone. "So are we. All we are trying to do is find out what happened to her."

He stared at me suspiciously but didn't reach for the phone.

"Do you have any idea where she was going on that Wednesday when she disappeared?" I asked.

He shook his head. "I only saw her on Tuesdays and Thursdays."

"What did she do after school on the other days?" I asked.

"I don't know. She had a lot of friends. I didn't want to ask her too many questions," he said, licking his lips nervously, "because she might have thought I was prying and not have come to see me anymore."

"What did you two do down here, anyway?" asked Jessie, looking with disgust at the dingy room.

Schuman gave her an equally disgusted look. I didn't think they were exactly hitting it off. His hand jerked spastically and ended up a little closer to the phone.

"What sorts of things did you talk about, Michael?" I asked.

He relaxed slightly. "We talked about books, about school and about our problems. I was teaching her how to play chess."

"What problems did she have?" I asked.

He shrugged his bony shoulders. The poor guy made me look overweight. "The usual, I guess. Grades, parents, friends, nothing special. Mostly she liked to help people but didn't think they really appreciated it."

"Do you have any names?" asked Jessie.

"Cathy liked to keep things private. She said that people wouldn't trust her if she told all their business to other people. That's why I talked to her. I knew it would be kept in confidence."

"Yeah, well, it's still pretty hard to believe that she never mentioned any names to you, if you were *really* such good friends," Jessie taunted.

"Are you calling me a liar?" Michael shouted suddenly, standing up to his full five feet six inches. In the quiet room his outburst made us both jump. Jessie even got off the desk and took a step back.

"We *were* friends. She said that she loved me, and I loved her. And I've had it with you two," he said fiercely, picking up the phone.

"We're going, we're going," I said desperately, pulling Jessie down the aisle to the door. I had to half drag her out into the hall.

I walked up the steps ahead of her, ignoring her calls to me, and returned the key to the desk. A little kid who looked uncomfortable grabbed it right away.

"What took you so long?" he muttered.

"I had to fight off a bat in the second stall. I think I killed it, but it may only be stunned," I said and walked out into the lobby without looking back.

Jessie caught up with me before I could reach the front door.

"What's the matter with you?" she asked, grabbing my arm and spinning me around.

"I don't know. I guess I just don't like working with a bully. I kept waiting for you to take out a baseball bat and threaten to smash his kneecaps."

"Well, I'm not too crazy about being with someone who pussyfoots around everyone like he's afraid of his own shadow," she shot back.

I took a deep breath, counted to ten, then to twenty and tried to sound reasonable. "All I'd like is for you to use a little tact, a smidgen of diplomacy, instead of pretending that you're a steamroller and everyone else is a little worm. Trying to scare information out of people isn't always the way to go."

She went out the door. I almost had to run to keep up, but even if our partnership was over, I needed a ride home. It was too far to walk.

At the car, I went around to the passenger's side, staring out at the darkness trying to ignore her, and waited for her to unlock the door.

"Lou," said a weak voice that barely sounded like Jessie's. There was something in the tone that made me turn.

Jessie was standing there with a small piece of paper in her hand, pointing at the windshield. There was a hole in the middle, and the safety glass had cracked in crazy patterns that almost covered the driver's side of the window.

A short, fat man getting into the car next to us noticed the damage and said, "That's a shame. There's so much vandalism around today. You should report it to the police. In fact, a police car was going through the lot when I arrived, but I guess they didn't see anything. That's the trouble with the police, they're never around when you need them."

When neither Jessie nor I answered him, he got into his car and drove off. I reached over and took the piece of paper from Jessie's unmoving hands.

THIS IS YOUR LAST WARNING! it said in large block letters. FORGET ABOUT CATHY!

"What happened to our first warning?" I asked nobody in particular.

Ten

We sat in the far booth of Mama Louisa's Italian Restaurant and Pizzeria. The waitress kept giving us funny looks. I don't know if it was because she thought we made an odd-looking couple or because we were both as white as sheets. Jessie had managed to drive by hunching forward in the seat and peering through the bottom part of the windshield which hadn't been shattered. We had both wanted to talk so I suggested Mama Louisa's. There's nothing like a pepperoni pizza to calm you down after a threat on your life.

Jessie insisted that we not talk about anything until the pizza came and we were relaxed. Otherwise, she said, we wouldn't be able to evaluate the situation objectively. I didn't think the situation needed any evaluating: it was bad, nothing but bad. But I didn't say anything until I had downed my first bite of pizza.

"Who could have given us that warning?" I blurted out.

Jessie almost choked and gave me an annoyed look. "It has to be somebody we've questioned. No one else would know," she answered finally.

"Unless one of them told somebody else, and that person was the one who did it. Maybe it's not likely, but it is possible," I concluded.

"Yeah, but if we leave that aside, the only people we've talked to are Mike at the gas station, Debbie, Rodger and Mike Schuman."

"Sure, but Mike Reynolds saw me looking under the desk, and I still say that we don't know who Julie and Naomi might have told."

"I'll check on that," said Jessie. I wouldn't want to be Julie or Naomi if Jessie found out that one of them had been talking.

"And don't forget," I continued, "you'd just insulted Mike Schuman. Maybe he did it only for spite."

"I doubt that he has the guts, and he didn't have the time," said Jessie dismissively, biting into another piece of pizza.

"Maybe he rode up on the dumbwaiter," I said, half joking.

Jessie eyed me suspiciously for a moment to see if I was serious. When I smiled, she decided I had been kidding and looked forlornly into the distance. "Why couldn't he have just left a note and not smashed the windshield?"

"That was to let us know he means business, assuming it is a he," I said. Remembering the kind of business he meant made me lose my appetite, and I put down my third slice of pizza. Suddenly it looked too much like blood and guts.

"But it told us something else," said Jessie with a triumphant smile. "Now we know for certain that Cathy didn't just decide to run away. Something happened to her, and someone wants to keep it hidden. I was right from the beginning!"

"Swell, so we'll both end up dead right. Whoever did kill her probably won't hesitate to do it again if we get too close," I said, still staring at the pizza.

"Are you okay?" she asked as I reached into my jacket pocket for a pack of cigarettes. My hand shook a little as I took one out and offered the pack to her.

"I don't smoke, and, anyway, I'm in training for track. Aren't you supposed to be training for baseball?" she asked, raising an eyebrow at me accusingly.

"Yeah, but nobody here knows me, and one cigarette won't hurt."

"Still, they're not good for your health," she insisted.

Having had enough hassles for one evening without a health lecture, I just smiled. "I didn't know you were on the track team. Somehow that doesn't seem like you."

"You mean, just because I look like a druggie or a hood, I can't be interested in sports? You should know by now, Dunlop, that I do what I like. The image other people have of me is their problem, not mine."

"Take it easy! You always get excited right away. You know, what I said in the library was true. You don't have enough patience to meet people halfway. Everything has to be a big fight. I didn't mean to insult you just now, and you'd know it if you paid a little attention. I think you look fine, and I guess being on the track team is what gives you such a great figure," I said without pausing for breath.

Jessie blushed—really!—and gave me a long look; then she simply said, "Thank you."

I grabbed a piece of cold pizza and began to chew. It's amazing how fast the cheese gets rubbery and the pepperoni starts to taste like redwood. I was still upset, what with the threat and fighting with Jessie, and the food was forming a big lump next to my heart. I figured that, when it got big enough, it would explode, and I'd be the first victim of pepperoni cardiac arrest.

"Phillips and Dunlop," she suddenly said loudly. "It has a nice ring to it. What do you think?"

"I'd prefer Dunlop and Phillips. It's more alphabetical. But I guess we should have age before beauty."

She laughed. It had an innocent, almost girlish, sound that I didn't expect, and I realized that this was the first time I had heard her really laugh. Maybe, even with all her self-confidence, she wasn't any happier than I was.

She took my hand, and her face became serious. "I know that I push kind of hard sometimes, but it's only because I want to get this thing over with. If you think it's time, maybe we should go to the police with what we know."

I sat there holding her hand as if it were the most natural thing in the world. Even though I was scared—a smashed windshield does that to me every time—I didn't like the idea of quitting just when we seemed to be getting somewhere.

"It's up to you," I finally answered, giving her hand a friendly squeeze, "but I still don't think we know enough. The police can write off the windshield as normal vandalism or as the result of a grudge somebody has against us for some other reason. And, unless we have something real good to tell them, they won't be very thrilled with us for going around trying to do their job for them. My father, for one, will have a fit."

"Okay," Jessie agreed, "I just wanted some reassurance. Seeing that note got me a little scared. I know I started this, but once in a while I think we may be in over our heads."

The idea of *my* reassuring *her* seemed kind of funny. But having done the reassuring, I had to admit to her that I didn't know what we should do next.

"I've been thinking," said Jessie, "that we should get a roster of all the students in the school and see how many have the name Mike. Maybe someone will ring a bell as having been a friend of Cathy's or a generally suspicious character."

I groaned. "Everybody seems to have been Cathy's friend, at least in secret. You know, I don't like to say it since she was a friend of yours and all, but I think she was kind of a tease.''

''What do you mean?''

''Well, she was friends with all these guys but never seemed to go out on a date with any of them. All they ever did was talk.''

''Not everyone is obsessed with sex,'' said Jessie, pulling away her hand, ''and she never promised them anything more than friendship.''

''Okay, but Mike at the gas station and Mike at the library were both guys with problems, and Cathy was more of an older sister or a mother to them than she was a girlfriend.''

''Sometimes mothering is a big part of being a girlfriend,'' Jessie replied.

''Yeah, but that's *all* it seems to have been for Cathy, and guys she picked were losers she was trying to help.''

''What's wrong with that?''

''All I'm saying,'' I said patiently, ''is that having all these secret boyfriends she was helping is a little strange.''

''There were only two as far as we know. I told you she was a romantic. I guess until the right guy came along she was more interested in just being friends with boys than in getting involved with them.''

"Maybe she wouldn't have known the right guy if she met him. Maybe she would have run away."

Jessie shrugged, so I gave up. "How are we going to get a school roster?" I asked, reaching out and taking her hand again. She didn't pull it away, so I figured that I was forgiven for having questioned Cathy's behavior.

"I know a girl who works in the office. She'll get it for me," Jessie answered.

"Another friend like Julie and Naomi?"

"Sort of."

"You sure have a lot of friends."

"That's because they admire my directness," she said, sipping her soda and looking up at me with big deep brown eyes that I could get lost in.

"Oh" was all I could gasp as her eyes met mine.

Marlowe tried to whisper something in the back of my mind, but I couldn't quite hear him over the thumping of my heart.

Eleven

Friday is always the best day of the school week because it's the last day, but this Friday was kind of boring. Jessie had told me last night that she was going to cut school today to get her windshield fixed, and sitting in English without her next to me made me realize how much I had looked forward to school lately because I could see her.

Another reason it was boring was that I could hardly stay awake on the little sleep I'd had It's easy to be calm about threats against your life when you're sitting in a crowded restaurant eating a pepperoni pizza, but home alone at night, things start

to look a little different. I actually got out of bed
five times to check on strange noises, and I kept my
eyes wide open in the dark, afraid to blink in case
someone came creeping through my bedroom door.
There's something personal about a threatening
note that can really get you on edge. I didn't fall
asleep until I heard my father come home. Sometimes—not often—it's nice to have a father who's
a cop.

Eric wasn't waiting for me in front of the school,
so I walked over to The Clearing alone. I didn't see
the crates, and since the sun had been out all day
and the ground was dry, I sat on a low mound of
earth at the far end. I still hadn't made up my mind
about the Virgin Islands. Getting away from it all
sounded like a great idea. Maybe Eric was right,
and the two of us could sell my father on the plan,
but I still wasn't sure that I wanted to travel on
someone else's money. Somehow the whole thing
just looked too easy; but then I told myself to stop
worrying. Why shouldn't things be easy for a
change?

"Get up!" Eric barked. He had walked into The
Clearing while I was thinking and now was standing there staring at me. I was so surprised at his or-
dering me around that I scrambled to my feet
almost before I knew what I was doing.

"What's the matter?" I asked. He looked kind of tense, and I wondered for a moment if he somehow knew that I had lied to him about investigating Cathy's disappearance.

Then he relaxed and smiled. His blue eyes sparkled. "I think that's where the hoboes used to dump their garbage. There are a lot of ants there."

I brushed off the seat of my pants. Even though it was for my own good, I was a little mad that he had shouted at me that way so I asked sharply, "What happened to the lousy crates?"

"I hid them here behind the bushes," Eric answered, hauling them out. "I was afraid that someone might come through here and take them. I know it's not likely, but you can't be too safe."

He offered me a cigarette, and we settled down on the boxes.

"I didn't see you yesterday," he said. "What happened? Baseball practice hasn't started already, has it?"

It sure gets hard keeping your lies straight once you start. "No, but we have to show up for calisthenics and tryouts." To change the subject I told him about seeing Mike Roeper being wheeled away.

"Yeah, he's just your typical subnormie," said Eric, flicking ash from his cigarette. "He can't cope with school or with life, so he pops himself full of pills and thinks the world's gonna go away.''

"I guess you're right," I began hesitantly, "but I've been thinking that maybe our trip to the Islands isn't much different."

"How do you mean?" he asked softly, giving me a closer look. You could never tell what he was thinking behind those light blue eyes.

"Well, you know, maybe I should get a job and start facing life, instead of traveling around on your money." I hadn't really meant to bring it up now or put it quite that way, but maybe it was just as well.

"Look, there's life and there's life. If you don't have to work eight hours a day in a factory in order to live, why do it?" he asked patiently.

I didn't say anything.

"People who don't have the brains or the money have to take jobs like that. We both have the brains and I have the money for both of us, so why waste your time with some stupid summer job? You'll learn plenty about life in the Islands," he said with a wink, "plus there's nothing wrong with having a good time."

"I know that, but..." I began, but Eric went on as if I hadn't said anything. He was excited and talked half to himself.

"Everyone envies people who don't have to follow the nine-to-five rat race. Look at television, especially those detective shows. The guy always lives in a beautiful part of the country, is his own boss, works whenever he feels like it and doesn't have a family tying him down. That's the good life. He's got everything that most of the poor suckers watching the show don't have, particularly his freedom."

"But it's not realistic," I objected. "That's only television."

Eric moved his hand as though brushing my comment away. "Of course, it's not easy, but it can be done. If you're smart and have enough self-discipline, you can lead whatever kind of life you want to live. But you need a plan, and you have to have priorities. Otherwise, you end up just following everyone else, another one of those poor sheep being led by a few special people."

Eric stared off into space as though he were continuing the discussion in silence with himself. I sat there feeling really confused. My confusion must have shown because, when Eric came back from wherever he was, he said, "Don't worry about it, Lou, just let me take care of it."

Twelve

Even though Easter vacation didn't start until next Friday, I got my usual prevacation interrogation that night, a week before it would start.

Dad: How many days do you have off?
Me: Four, including the weekend.
Dad: What are you going to do with your time?
Me: I have lots of homework to do.
Dad: Not four days' worth. I don't want you hanging out down in the center of town just watching the traffic go by.

Me: Well, I have to get in shape for baseball season. I figured I'd do some running and maybe work out down at the Y.

Apparently this was a good answer because he nodded approvingly and said, "If you get a chance, rake up some of the leaves and branches in the yard."

It's amazing how easy a conversation can be if you only plan ahead. I knew that giving him the baseball permission slip to sign before dinner had been a good idea.

Later that evening, however, without planning ahead at all, I called Jessie and asked her out to a movie.

"Tonight?" she asked in an odd tone.

"Yeah, I know it's kind of short notice, but..." I sort of let the sentence fade away.

"But you figured that I wouldn't have anything else to do," Jessie finished the sentence.

"No! That's not it at all," I protested.

"And I bet you don't have a car, so you want *me* to pick *you* up?"

"Well...maybe we should forget it," I said reluctantly.

I didn't expect the laughter that almost blew out my eardrum.

"I'm just giving you a hard time. I'll pick you up around seven," she said through her laughter.

"Sure. Fine," I mumbled. Was the whole world crazy? I wondered. I guess you can't prepare for everything.

Right at seven she pulled up at the curb, and I hopped in.

"I was going to park and go up and ring the bell, but I didn't want to get our sex roles confused," she said, jamming the car into gear.

"No fear of that," I said, and we both smiled a little.

"I see you got the windshield fixed."

"Yeah, and I was lucky they had one in stock. Otherwise, I'd have had to wait while they sent one over from Germany."

"You haven't gotten any more threats, have you?" I asked after a moment.

"No, but remember, the note said that it was the last one."

Neither of us spoke. I think we were both still trying to absorb exactly what that meant.

"Say, are you paying for this?" she asked suddenly.

"Of course, I asked you out."

"Yeah, I keep trying to remember that. I guess that means you get to choose the movie, but if you don't mind, I'd like to go to that cut-rate place on the other side of town."

"I can afford to pay full price," I grumbled.

"I know, but I want to see the movie playing there."

I said that was fine, and we talked about the movie for a while. Jessie told me about training for track and asked me why I decided to go out for baseball. I started to tell her that it was all really just because of a lie that I had told Eric, then I started to explain that I only did it to get my father off my back. But then I realized that in some strange way I did want to be on the team, and I tried to explain that to her.

She nodded. "Sure, it's a way of expressing yourself, of showing who you are. Know what I mean?"

I didn't answer. Between Jessie and Eric, I'd had about enough of this topic. Tonight I just wanted to have a good time.

But Jessie was on her soapbox. "A lot of people—parents, teachers, even other kids—try to keep you from being yourself. It's funny, but Mrs. Hiller, the art teacher, is one of the worst ones."

"You have Heil Hiller for art?" I said, gasping. The joke around school was that, instead of college, all her training came from being a prison guard. She was a tall, muscular woman, who spoke with a faint accent and never smiled. The kids always gave her the Nazi salute behind her back. You know, the arm straight out like you see in the old movies about Hitler.

Her idea of creativity was to do it her way. She would always say, "There will be enough time to do it your own way after you learn how to do it the right way."

"Yeah," Jessie answered, "and she gives everyone the same boring project. Draw a hand! Sketch a tree! Diagram the school! You never get to express yourself."

In spite of not wanting to talk about it, I said, "But maybe it's important to learn the right way to do things."

"Sure, but you can't go on doing copies all your life. Eventually you have to stop doing imitations and show what you can do."

I grunted and stared out the window. Even Jessie got the hint and let the subject drop.

After a few minutes she said softly, "That's where Cathy lived," and pointed to a large white ranch house on the left side of the road.

I went back to wondering if the time would ever come for me to really be myself. Then suddenly it came to me like one of those stupid light bulbs that go on over the heads of cartoon characters.

"Jessie, we're blind!" I shouted.

"Huh, what do you see?" she asked, peering out into the darkness.

"We never bothered to ask ourselves why Cathy walked in the *opposite* direction from home every day," I said excitedly.

Jessie frowned "Well, we know she went to the library to see Schuman on Tuesdays and Thursdays."

"Yeah, but what about the other days? Mike saw her go by the gas station every day, and he had no reason to lie about that. That's in the opposite direction from her house, and she never showed up at the Burger Shack before four-thirty. Where did she go from two forty-five to four o'clock on Mondays, Wednesdays and Fridays from September until she disappeared?"

"It had to be somewhere that nobody from school usually goes, and Debbie took her in that same direction on the last day she was seen. Somewhere that nobody knew about."

"Someone else knew about it, and that's the person who knows what happened to her."

Jessie began to beat on the steering wheel in time to the music on the radio. "All we do is get deeper and deeper into the mystery, but it never seems to get any clearer."

"Once you get to the middle of the forest, you're already on the way out," I said confidently.

"You know, sometimes you sound like a fortune cookie. When you're not sounding like a Grade B movie, that is," she said.

"Well, I guess that's your good fortune, sweetheart," I growled in my best imitation of a tough guy.

She didn't say anything, but in the glow of the dashboard lights, I could tell that she was smiling. I maintained a dignified silence all the way to the movie. It was in one of those large theaters that had been divided into four separate cinemas about ten years ago. The movie we wanted was playing in Cinema Four.

"In my day movie houses had real names like The Rivoli, The Bijou or The Roxy," grumbled Marlowe in the back of my mind. "Now they all have the same name and a number. Pretty soon it will be the same with people."

Yeah, and in the old days they put real butter on the popcorn, I thought. You know, sometimes you can be kind of a grouch, Marlowe.

We sat in the back, sharing a box of stale popcorn with phony butter, and waited for the show to begin. Jessie reached into her bag and handed me several pieces of paper stapled together.

"What's this?"

"It's a list of all the students in the high school. Why don't you enjoy yourself over the weekend by going through the Mikes to see if any seem to be likely suspects we haven't talked to yet," said Jessie.

I was about to complain that partners usually divided the work, when I saw Rodger come in with three other people. One of them was Bud Metcalf, a giant lineman on the football team. Murderin' Metcalf, as he was called, had a body like an oak and a brain like an acorn. They had two girls with them. I started to nudge Jessie, but she was already watching them intently.

"Why's Rodger with that Metcalf jerk?" I asked.

"The girl Rodger's with is Bud's sister, Pamela."

Pamela looked kind of cute from a distance. I guess you can never tell how the genes will bounce.

Rodger looked back and saw us looking at him, then he whispered something to Bud, who managed to turn his mountain of a body around to stare at us. I didn't wave; I figured it might antagonize him. After a while everyone got tired of staring, and things settled down. The movie still hadn't started yet; I discovered that the sight of Rodger and Bud together had given me a strong desire to go to the bathroom, so I excused myself and went to the rest room in the lobby.

They came in behind me. Just like a disgusting disease, Rodger stood there smiling, and Bud did an excellent imitation of a concrete wall. Rodger nodded, and The Wall pinned my arms behind my back.

"So you're still spying on me, Dunlop? I warned you about that. You're going to go running to Debbie and tell her you saw me with someone else?"

Somehow I didn't think denying it would help, plus he didn't give me a chance. Rodger started to pull his right fist back and took a short step toward me to get within range. Using Bud for support, I kicked forward with all I had and caught Rodger on the right shin. He yelped and began to swear and groan while hobbling around like a pirate with a peg leg.

"Kill him, Bud!" he shouted, when he finally caught his breath.

Bud half spun, half threw me across the room into the urinals. The last thing I saw was the white procelain rushing up to meet me like a snowbank.

It was a peaceful island. There was a waterfall splashing softly, gently lulling me to sleep as I lay on the ground nearby. There was the smell of pine in the air but also an aroma that suggested there might be a swamp in the neighborhood. A beautiful native girl in colorful clothes was bending over me and softly stroking my head. I guessed that Eric and I had finally made our trip. I was very happy and knew there was a big, silly smile on my face.

But something was wrong. The girl looked like Jessie, and even I didn't think that native girls were blonde. Also, this girl was throwing icy water on my face. I *knew* island girls weren't supposed to do that!

"Wake up, Lou. Come on! Please!" an insistent voice was shouting. This was no island girl.

I turned away to admire the waterfall and saw the water splashing into the bottom of a broken urinal. I sat up. Too fast. I lay down again and started over slowly. Finally I focused on Jessie, who was leaning over me with a worried expression on her face.

"You're going to have a nasty bump there," she said, rubbing a spot near the top of my head so vigorously that I took her hand away. "What happened?"

I explained as best I could about The Wall falling on me.

"What are you doing in here?" I asked.

"I saw the two of them go out to the lobby after you, then come back in a hurry a few minutes later, grab the girls and almost run out. When you didn't show up, I figured that I'd better investigate," she explained.

A little boy walked in, took one look at Jessie and rushed out, calling for his mother.

"You shouldn't be in here," I said, trying to stand.

"Bull," she said calmly.

I didn't have an answer to that.

"You could have a concussion. Maybe we should go to the hospital for X rays."

"If you want some, fine, but I don't need any. If my father ever found out, then I'd really need them."

Jessie helped me to my feet. I threw some cold water on my face and neck and tried not to look in the mirror. But I did catch a glimpse of my face. Not bad for the living dead.

We went out to the lobby. The old woman selling phony popcorn stared at Jessie with her mouth twisted as if she had just eaten a lemon. We decided to skip the movie, and Jessie drove me home.

Although I think she was almost bursting to ask some questions, Jessie kept quiet during the ride and I kept conscious. When we pulled up in front of my house, all she asked was whether I would be all right alone and if I needed help to get inside. I bravely told her that I'd be fine.

The talk died out, and suddenly we were just looking at each other. Maybe it was the bump on my head, but everything seemed different, sort of far away.

Finally, with a little smile, she said, "You can come closer. I won't bite."

And she didn't.

Thirteen

The next morning I felt pretty good, except for a sore spot on the top of my head. When I thought about Jessie, even that felt a lot better. Since it was Saturday, my father was sleeping later, but soon he would get up and then prowl around the house for the rest of the day, making my life miserable. I didn't feel up to dodging questions. Because it was too nice a day to hole up in my room and pretend to study, I decided to go over to Oglethorp's. I was at the door when Jessie called to see how I was. I told her I felt fine and asked if we could talk things over on Monday. Even though I wanted to talk to her longer, I hung up fast before my father woke up and started wondering who was on the phone.

Taking care of Oglethorp's yard was my father's one small concession to the fact that I was over ten. I was complaining one day about needing a job in order to have some money of my own, and he said he knew this retired prep school teacher who wanted someone to mow the lawn, shovel snow, rake leaves and that sort of thing. I think my father admired the old guy and thought that, being a former teacher and all, he'd be a good influence on me. What a joke!

Oglethorp was a drunk. Oh, sure, there were lots of times when he was sober as a judge, sometimes for a month or more, but then he would go on a bender, and you'd hardly see him for weeks. Actually, it was better not to see him when he was that way. I knew that from experience.

Last summer, about the second time I'd worked there, I'd needed more gas for the lawn mower and knocked on the front door to get some money. I hadn't seen Oglethorp around that day, but I figured he might be home—you can't always tell with old people. I heard him shout "Coming! Coming!" Looking through the narrow windows in the door, I saw him weave down the front hall, bouncing from one wall to the other like a crazy pinball.

Finally he reached the door and, after fumbling with the lock for what seemed like hours, got it open.

I tried to explain about the gasoline and said that I'd come back later, but he shouted, "Come right in, boy! Come right in!" and pulled me into the hallway by the arm. After repeating my story about the gasoline a couple more times while he leaned against the wall and blew his nose, the information seemed to sink in. "Follow me!" he ordered and found his way into the living room, where he pulled open the top drawer of an old desk that sat in one corner. The drawer came all the way out and everything fell out on the ratty carpet. He bent over and picked this flat tin box out of the mess, as though this was the normal way to get something out of a drawer. Then he staggered over to an old stuffed chair and flopped down. He sat there with the tin in his hand and stared at the floor. I figured he'd forgotten what he was doing and was about to tell my gasoline tale again for the tenth time, when he looked up and said, "It's lousy getting old."

I almost said that it was better than the alternative but figured that this wasn't the time for humor.

"Yeah, it's really lousy. Your body doesn't do what you want it to do."

He stared up at me, so I tried to nod sympathetically.

"And all you think about is dying. I don't want to die," he said as though this was supposed to come as a surprise to me.

"Nobody does," I answered automatically.

"The old want to live more than the young because it's become such a habit for them."

He motioned for me to come closer and fumbled with the lid of the tin. It came off, and some change and a ten-dollar bill fell into his lap. He picked up the ten dollars and pulled me closer. I started to pull away, but he held me tightly and stuffed the bill into my shirt pocket.

"Keep the change," he said with a drunken grin and released my arm.

"Thanks," I said and rushed out.

A few days later I mailed the change back to him. I figured he wasn't really in his right mind when he gave it to me. We never talked about what had happened, and I certainly never told my father. I didn't want to lose the only job he'd let me have. Plus, when he was sober, Oglethorp could be a pretty cool guy. He didn't treat you like you were a kid, you know. He would tell you what he really thought about something and not just give you some line he thought kids were supposed to hear.

He even had a weird sense of humor that was pretty neat. One time during the winter when I came to shovel snow late one afternoon, he stuck his head out the window and recited:

The woods are lovely, dark and deep,
But you have promises to keep;
And miles to shovel before you sleep,
And miles to shovel before you sleep.

Thanks to Kasterson's class, I knew that was Oglethorp's version of a poem by a guy named Robert Frost, and in a way it was kind of funny, especially seeing this old guy with white hair blowing all around, yelling out the window during a snowstorm.

This time when I got there, Oglethorp was out behind the house wearing a pair of baggy khaki pants and a sweater with holes in the elbows. I breathed a sigh of relief because he wouldn't be puttering around out here if he were drunk, and I wanted to collect what he owed me for last month. He had a pair of small shears in his hand and was talking to himself as he cut back the grape vines. He looked up as I walked across the yard.

"I should have done this in February before the sap started to run," he muttered, cutting off a long branch covered with buds.

"Hey! Are you sure you're supposed to cut off all those buds? How's it going to have any grapes this year?"

"It wouldn't have many if I didn't," he answered, lopping off still more. "I know it looks cruel or stupid, but unless you keep the plant down to a few main vines, all its energy goes into making branches and not enough into growing grapes."

I gave him a close look to make sure he was sober, but his eyes weren't red, his speech wasn't slurred and his hands didn't shake. He looked back at me and straightened to look me in the eye, as though he knew what I was thinking. At first he seemed a little irritated, but when he started to talk again, his voice was patient and soft.

"You see, it's like a lot of things in life. You have to make some hard choices. You can't do everything you want to do, be everything you want to be or be everything other people want you to be. You've got to decide, and whichever way you go, something is going to be lost."

I couldn't believe that I was standing there listening to advice on life from someone who probably only knew what day it was if his social security check came through the mail slot. Everybody seemed to be telling me about making hard decisions as if it were the easiest thing in the world to do. Maybe I had to listen when it came from people like Eric or Jessie, but a drunk like Oglethorp was something else.

"So what did you ever decide to do with your life?" I didn't mean it to sound sarcastic, but I guess it did a little because I got another long look. Then he nodded and rearranged the wrinkles on his face into a small smile.

"You're right, I've made some wrong choices, but you learn more from mistakes than you do from successes, so maybe I know what I'm talking about. Remember," he said, giving the vine a vicious chop, "the future isn't going to be much different from the present, so you'd better start right now being the kind of person you want to be or else you never will."

I didn't say anything. I walked to the garage, got a plastic yard bag and a rake and started putting some piled-up leaves in the bag. Most of the time when I thought of the future, it made me happy. It had to be better than school and being a kid. But just for a moment, as I pushed the leaves down into the black mouth of the bag, I thought of the future and was afraid.

Fourteen

We were hiding in our usual corner across from the clinic. Inside, the nurse was calmly holding a girl's head down so that she wouldn't faint at the sight of the blood dripping from her finger; at the same time she was telling the dentist where to set up his equipment to conduct the yearly dental check. I've always wondered what the point is of these yearly exams by the doctor and dentist. It's all such a production line that about the only thing they find out is that you're alive and have teeth.

Jessie was still angry about what had happened at the movie theater and kept insisting that I turn Bud and Rodger in to the police.

"I don't think what they did had anything to do with Cathy's disappearance," I said patiently. "If we bring the police in on this, pretty soon they'll find out that we've been asking questions, and then we'll be in trouble."

"I don't see how you can be so sure that Rodger isn't involved with whatever happened to Cathy," Jessie whispered fiercely as two girls walked by.

"I'm not sure, but he seemed more worried about Debbie finding out that he's going out with Metcalf's sister than anything else."

"Debbie probably knows about Pam already. Just like she knows about all the others."

"It could be that she suspects," I agreed, "but Rodger still wouldn't want anyone going to her with hard facts. I think he wants to keep her and at the same time go out with anyone else who looks interesting."

"He's a real creep. I'd almost like to tell her, just to foul up his lousy little game."

"Go ahead, and you can visit me in the hospital. I'll be the one in traction, bandaged from head to toe like a mummy," I said a little angrily.

Jessie reached over and took my hand. "Yeah, I guess I'll forget that idea. Sorry."

I accepted the apology and held on to her hand. "I looked through the school roster over the weekend," I said, "but nobody named Mike, aside from the ones we've checked, had any special connection with Cathy that I can think of."

"Yeah, I skimmed the list before I gave it to you. There are about a thousand guys in the school and at least fifty Mikes. It could be any one of them," concluded Jessie sadly.

"Or maybe none of them?" I asked, suddenly inspired.

"Huh? Oh, you mean it could be the Mike at the garage."

"No," I said. "I was just thinking. Cathy was the romantic sort, right?"

Jessie agreed.

"Well, why would she plaster the guy's name on all her desks but hide it under the table in home ec?"

"Maybe she didn't want everyone at the table to see it," suggested Jessie.

"Okay, but why do it at all, then? Why go down on your hands and knees to put it under a table where only a midget would see it?"

"What are you getting at?"

"Just this: if somebody went to the trouble of erasing his name from all those hearts on Cathy's desks, why not plant a phony one in case somebody got suspicious and started to investigate?" I finished triumphantly.

Jessie stared thoughtfully into the clinic where the dentist was struggling to set up his chair. "So the guy, whoever he is, just used the name Mike to throw people off the track. But why not put it on top of the table or on one of the desks?"

"Maybe he thought it would be too obvious. Somebody might wonder how Cathy could be putting hearts on desks a month after she had disappeared. What I don't know is why he picked the table in home ec."

"Maybe he had a class in there?"

"Could be. About the only guys it couldn't be are those named Mike. It really throws a monkey wrench into everything we've done so far."

"There is one thing we haven't checked that might help," said Jessie slowly.

"What?"

"Her gym locker. If some guy has been going around erasing his name from her hearts, that would be the hardest place for him to get to," said Jessie. "I should have thought of it sooner, but when you found the heart with Mike in it, I thought we had the answer."

"Hmm. Do you know which locker she used?"

"Not offhand, but we had gym together, and Mrs. Hernandes puts the locker numbers next to the names in her attendance book at the beginning of the year. Cathy's name and number are probably still there. If I can get a look at that book, I'm pretty sure I can find out what locker she used." A mischievous glint came into Jessie's eyes. "I'll sneak into her office during class, I'll say I have to go to the bathroom or something, and peek in the book."

"Be careful!" I warned as we separated to go to class.

She winked. "Don't worry about me."

"That's my kind of woman," Marlowe whispered in the back of my mind.

She's mine, I answered.

Probably because I was walking on air as I went down the hall, I didn't see Marty Stanton until I bumped into him.

"Hey," he said with a laugh, "you aren't going to be the next one we have to take out in a wheelchair, are you?"

"Nope, this is a purely natural high."

"Good. I was afraid after our last talk that things were getting you down. I know it's hard when something happens to someone you know, but we did everything we could for Cathy."

"You make it sound like you're a doctor, and she was a patient you lost in surgery."

Marty suddenly looked very sad. "I guess in a way the jobs are alike, especially with a missing-person's case. You always think that, if you had just done things right, the kid would be back in school and with her family. That the whole problem would be cured."

"No doctor saves all his patients," I said, trying to cheer him up.

"And no cop solves all his cases," he said softly and walked slowly away from me down the hall.

Eric was already there when I reached The Clearing that afternoon. He had his shirt off and was lying in a patch of warm sunlight that filtered through the trees. The yellow sun made his blond hair glow as if it were on fire. If it had been me lying there, it would look more like a slab of white meat with some mousy brown hair on top. Some people are born with it all. They naturally look and act special. That's the way it is.

I moved and broke a twig. Eric turned.

"A great day for soaking up some sun," he said. "It really gets the cobwebs out of your system."

"I know what you mean," I agreed, flopping down next to him. "It's great to be outside again."

"Yeah, well, we'll have more sun than we can handle this summer in the Caribbean," he said, closing his eyes.

I hadn't been thinking much about my own problems today. I'd been too busy trying to solve the case. But suddenly I knew what I had to say to Eric.

"I've been thinking about our trip," I began slowly. "Maybe you're right about it being a good idea, but I don't want you paying my way, even if you can afford it. If we go anywhere, it will have to be somewhere that I can afford, and I'll be the one to talk my father into it."

Eric continued to lie there with his eyes closed as though I hadn't said a thing. Finally he said, "Okay."

"Is that all?"

"Sure. I offered to pay your way. If you won't take it, then that's the way it is."

I couldn't tell if he was angry or not. I really did want to go somewhere with him over the summer, so I said, "I have about two hundred saved up from taking care of Oglethorp's place, and I'll get more from a job my father is going to get me washing cars down at the station."

"I suppose we could get a place at the shore for a week. A poor man's holiday," he said in a dead voice.

I sat staring at the ground. Maybe I was just afraid to take a chance, as Eric was always saying, and this money thing was only an excuse. Jessie worried because she thought nothing was happening, while I always worried because too much was happening. Isn't anybody ever satisfied?

Without opening his eyes, Eric said, "I'm disappointed because we've been talking about taking a real trip for so long that I was really looking forward to it."

"Yeah, so was I." Sort of, I thought.

He propped himself up on one elbow and gave me a faint smile. "I suppose we could have a pretty good time at the shore, and I know some people who own a beach house that maybe we could rent cheap. I guess the Caribbean will just have to wait until next year."

"Sure, it'll still be there," I said with relief, "and by then I'll have more money. Maybe I can get my father to let me find a job for after school next year."

"Yeah, but remember you still have to talk him into the trip this year," Eric warned.

"I'll take care of that," I said with more confidence than I really felt.

Fifteen

It turned out to be harder than Jessie had expected to discover Cathy's locker number. Coach Hernandes almost never let the book out of her sight because she used it to keep track of which students got dressed for gym, whether they were late and if they actually played or only pretended to play some sport. A couple of days went by before Jessie could convince the coach that she wanted to check how many times she hadn't dressed for gym. And while Hernandes carefully went down the list to Jessie's name, Jessie looked over her shoulder and found Cathy's locker number.

Jessie tried to inspect the locker after gym, but the next class was coming in and there was no time. So on the Thursday afternoon before the Easter break, we were sneaking down the hall to the girls' gym. It's hard to sneak anywhere at three o'clock in the afternoon, and although most of the teachers had left, we had to be careful to avoid the janitors and vice principals who would stop anyone who looked suspicious. I don't know if I looked suspicious, but I certainly felt that way.

"You stay here and let me know if anyone's coming," Jessie ordered as we stopped outside the locker room door.

"No! If anyone sees me standing here, outside the girls' locker room, they'll be coming and quick. It's better if I stand inside and peek out the door," I suggested nervously.

"Okay, but keep your eyes open. The janitor is going to be coming along to lock the place up soon. We don't have to worry, the door won't be locked on the inside, but I don't want him to see the lights on and get curious."

There was a light switch next to the door, and since there were no windows for the light to be seen through, Jessie flipped them on and quickly headed back to where Cathy's locker was located. I remained by the door. All I needed was a uniform and I'd be a great doorman, like the ones they have at fancy hotels and apartments. Imagine how boring it must be to hold the door and hail taxis for people all day.

"Yeah, and hoping that someone will do you a big favor and give you a quarter for a tip," whispered Marlowe in the back of my mind.

I thought I heard a noise and opened the door a crack to peer out, but there was nothing. It was probably just my worrier's imagination.

"Lou, come with me for a minute," Jessie whispered into my ear. I almost leaped into the air and did a double flip. Wearing sneakers instead of her usual noisy boots, she had almost given me a heart attack.

I followed her to the rear of the room. We stopped in front of K-19. The lockers don't have locks of their own on them. The kid is supposed to take the padlock from her gym basket and use it on the locker while she's in class to keep her regular clothes secure. After class the lock goes back on her basket with the gym clothes in it, which meant that at this time of day all the lockers were open. Jessie pointed to a small heart on the inside of the door of K-19. It was exactly like all the other hearts that Cathy had drawn, except this one had two names inside: Cathy loves Palindrome.

"Who the heck's Palindrome?" I asked.

"Beats me. It's certainly an odd name. If I'd ever heard it before, I'm sure I would remember it. Sounds like one of those names a knight would have in the Middle Ages, you know, 'Sir Lancelot, I'd like you to meet Sir Palindrome.'"

I heard the door to the locker room swing open, but before I could do any more than put my hand up to motion Jessie to be quiet, the lights went out. Even though I couldn't see a thing, I was certain that we were both looking at each other, wondering what to do next. I could feel the blackness pressing up against my eyeballs as I stood there wondering whether eating more carrots would have helped in a situation like this. Funny the things that go through your mind sometimes.

Footsteps came down the center aisle. They came slowly. Whoever it was didn't seem to care if we heard him, and that scared me even more. "Move up against the lockers," I whispered to Jessie as the steps got closer to our row. I heard a soft shuffle as she slid over to the side.

Before I could move over to the wall myself, the footsteps reached the end of our row and stopped. Whoever it was now stood only about twenty feet away, so I froze. There was no sound from any of us. It was like one of those war movies where the submarine is being bombarded by a destroyer with depth charges, so the whole crew of the sub has to be real quiet. The destroyer knew we were there but not exactly where. I tried to breathe softly and felt as if I were suffocating. I really wanted to take a huge lungful of air and shout, "Here we are! Now what are you going to do!" But instead I calmed down, began to breathe normally and hoped he wouldn't hear my heart pounding.

Suddenly I heard a small grunt of effort. Something behind me at the end of the row exploded, and a second later I vaguely heard the locker room door open and close with a soft hiss.

A few seconds that seemed like hours went by. "Are you all right?" Jessie whispered in a trembling voice.

I nodded and then realized she couldn't see that. "Yeah, I'm okay. Do you think he's gone?"

"I heard the door open. I think he left."

"Well, I guess the only way to be sure is to turn on the light." I started walking toward the main aisle. There was no one waiting there when I reached it. I went along slowly with my hands out in front of me since I didn't want to use my nose to discover a locker door or a wall. After what seemed like days, I felt the switch and turned on the lights.

When I got back to Jessie, she was holding a black disk in her hand and staring at it as though she were in some kind of daze.

"What's that?" I asked.

She didn't answer me, so I reached over and took it out of her hand. Its heaviness surprised me, and I almost dropped it. Ten Pounds it said on the side. It was a weight, the kind used on the barbells in the weight room down the hall.

"Look at the locker," Jessie said in a funny voice and collapsed on a nearby bench.

The metal door was bulging away from the hinges, and it looked as if it had been kicked in, but high up, above where anyone's foot could reach. Slowly it dawned on me that someone had thrown this heavy thing. My legs got a weak, wobbly feeling, and I ended up on the bench next to Jessie.

"That could have killed one of us, you know," she said.

"Maybe, but I think that whoever chucked it purposely threw high."

"Then why throw it?"

"Just to scare us."

"It worked."

I had to agree with her there.

"Who do you think threw it?"

"Probably whoever sent us our last warning in front of the library," I said. "It could be this guy Palindrome."

"But why give us a second warning? Why not go for the kill?" Jessie asked logically.

Sometimes I wished she wouldn't be so logical. "Haven't you heard of not looking gift horses in the mouth?"

"Huh?"

"Let's just say this guy Palindrome was feeling charitable today and leave it at that."

"You don't have to get grouchy," Jessie snapped.

"Almost being killed makes me sort of irritable. Sorry."

"Okay, but we've got to get out of here before the janitor comes around," Jessie said, leaping to her feet. Nothing seemed to keep her down for long. I followed her out of the building through the side door.

It was good to be in the sunlight and fresh air. Standing out there with the green grass and birds singing, it almost seemed that no one had tried to kill us in the land of sneakers and dirty sweat socks.

"We have to find out who this Palindrome is," said Jessie urgently, grabbing my arm. "Check your school roster tonight and see if anyone has that name. We have to find him before he takes another shot.''

"And you're the target," Marlowe whispered in my mind.

Sixteen

Hey Dad," I said that evening at supper, "I was thinking the other day about what I might do over the summer." I tried to sound as upbeat as possible.

His expression didn't change. "I thought you were going to work down at the station washing the cruisers?"

"Oh, sure, I'm still going to do that, but I was thinking that toward the end of vacation I might go away for a couple of weeks."

"Go away where?" he asked with a hard note of suspicion creeping into his tone.

"Oh, down to the shore. Eric and I thought we'd get a small place near the beach for a couple of weeks, just to relax."

"Relax!" he said sarcastically. "I didn't think you did enough during the year to need to relax. And I know what kids do down there. I'd have to come down and bail you out before you even got your bathing suit wet."

"We just want to swim a little and lie in the sun."

"Forget it!"

"Why should I?" My voice started to rise.

"Okay, don't get all excited. I'll talk it over with Eric and see what we can work out."

Maybe it was the picture of my father and Eric deciding what to do with me, as if I were a little kid, that did it. I'm not sure, but something snapped.

"Don't humor me!" I shouted. "If you talk it over with anyone, it's going to be with me. Do you understand?"

He didn't say anything, but his mouth sagged a little. I got up and walked to my room as calmly as I could. For once he didn't stop by to pat me on the head when he left.

"I found out about Palindrome!" Jessie said breathlessly over the phone. "You'll never believe it!"

Still numb from my argument with my father, all I could say was, "So who's Palindrome?"

"Are you all right? You sound funny."

"Yeah, I'm great. Now who's this Palindrome guy?"

"It's not a who, it's a what!" Jessie announced proudly.

"What are you talking about?"

"A palindrome is a word, sentence or number that reads the same backward or forward. The name Otto, for instance, is spelled the same either way, and the number 77 reads the same when reversed."

"How did you find all this out?" Curiosity was overcoming my bad mood.

"I thought Palindrome sounded like the name of a character in a book, and we know how much Cathy liked to read. So I looked in this dictionary of literary names and terms that they have in the library. Palindrome isn't the name of a character like I thought, but it is a term," concluded Jessie, obviously pleased with herself.

"So you think Cathy's boyfriend had a name that was spelled the same when reversed, so she called him Palindrome just to be cute."

"It sounds like something Cathy would do."

"Great," I said, "but nobody's named Otto anymore. How many other names does it work with?"

Jessie's voice dropped in disappointment. "Well, it works with Mom, Dad and Sis."

"Even Cathy wasn't weird enough to be drawing hearts for her father," I said sharply.

Jessie was quiet for a moment, probably trying to find the patience to go on.

"The only other ones I can think of are girls' names—Ana, Nan and Lil."

"Wait a minute!" I shouted, starting to get into the spirit of the game. "What about Bob?"

"Sure, that works!"

"Yeah, but do you know how many guys have that name? It's almost as bad as Mike. Plus we don't know of one Bob who knew Cathy really well."

We were both silent for a few moments, mentally going through the alphabet, looking for other possibilities.

"I can't think of any other boys' names that work," I concluded, discouraged.

"Neither can I," Jessie admitted. "Hey!" she said a second later. "Maybe it isn't a first name we're looking for at all, but a last name. You have the school roster. Why don't you look at the last names and see if any guy's name works? I'll hold on.''

I went up to my room, got the list and picked up the extension in my father's room. As I went through each letter, I reported to Jessie, "No A's, no B's . . ." She groaned each time. I went through a few more letters. Then I saw it and quietly hung up the phone. I knew who Palindrome was and all the pieces came together.

I walked into the bathroom and looked at my face in the mirror. I don't know how long I stood there staring, wondering how I could still look the same knowing what I did now.

Then the doorbell rang. For a moment I was going to ignore it, but the bell rang again and again. All I wanted to do was stop it from ringing.

I pulled open the door, and there stood Jessie. She looked as though she couldn't decide whether to be worried or angry.

"What happened to you? Are you all right? You just hung up all of a sudden without saying anything."

"I'm fine," I said coldly, standing in the doorway. "I accidentally hit the button on the phone. I was going to call you back."

"Well, now you don't have to," she said with a smile, slipping past me into the living room.

I slammed the door.

"Look, I think you'd better leave. I have a lot of things to do tomorrow, and my father doesn't like me to have people in the house when he isn't home."

"You didn't say anything about that the other night when you had me over. Then you were the grown-up man. Now, all of a sudden, you're the little boy who has to listen to his father."

She didn't exactly say it in a mocking tone, but I could feel the anger starting as a tightness in the back of my neck.

She continued in a level voice. "You've found out something. Tell me what it is."

None of this would have happened if she hadn't wanted to discover what had happened to Cathy, a girl I hardly knew. It was all Jessie's fault. If I hadn't listened to her, everything would still be fine. The anger, frustration and unfairness of it all made my head feel like it was exploding. I reached out and grabbed Jessie by the jacket and began to force her toward the door.

"Leave, just leave!" I shouted.

She pulled back in surprise, and my hand caught under the collar of her shirt and ripped it open. A button popped off and lay on the carpet between us. I slumped down on the sofa. Jessie stood over me, not even trying to hold her shirt together. After a few moments she stooped down and picked up the button.

"I guess this is one of those times when I should have been more tactful," she finally said. "But let me tell you, fella, your own approach needs a lot of work."

"I'm sorry. You're right. Right about everything. I do know something, but I've got to work it out my own way before I tell anyone."

"Even me?"

I nodded miserably.

After a few seconds, while I guess she was deciding whether to argue the point, she said, "Okay. But as soon as you're sure, let me know. Remember, this is my case, too."

Again I nodded. She left, closing the door quietly.

"You've got a job to do, kid," Marlowe whispered in my mind, as I went to the phone to call Palindrome. And for the third time that night I nodded.

Seventeen

I was waiting when he got to The Clearing. The sun had warmed the ground, and I wanted to lie down and sleep. Since it was the Friday before Easter, there was no school, and I'd spent most of the morning just wandering around town, walking down by the river and not noticing much of anything around me. I was tired. Tired of walking, and tired of trying to figure out what had gone wrong.

He came strolling through the woods, whistling, and waved as he entered The Clearing. "How's it going? I didn't expect to see you today. How come you called? It all sounded pretty mysterious,'' he said, sitting on the ground next to me.

"I had to talk to you."

"Talk away," Eric said, turning his face up toward the sun.

I took a deep breath but could still hear the blood pounding in my ears.

"I followed through on Cathy's disappearance, even though I told you I wasn't going to," I said flatly and remembered how important it had once seemed to keep this fact a secret from him. What a fool I had been. "I think I know what happened to her."

Eric didn't move. He didn't even look, but a small twitch started in the right corner of his mouth.

I went on. "I think that there was something going on between you and Cathy and that the two of you used to meet here on Mondays, Wednesdays and Fridays. On the last day she was seen alive, I think she told you about Mike at the garage, and you got angry, killed her somehow and hid the body. Then a few weeks later you started bringing me here." The twitch had gotten worse at the mention of Mike's name.

"Anything else?" he asked softly.

"Lots more. On the last day, Cathy got out of Debbie's car by the railroad tracks. At first I thought she was going across to the gas station, but now I think she planned to come here and have it out with you. And Hannah spelled backward is still Hannah, so when Cathy drew all those hearts saying that she loved Palindrome, she meant you. Of course you knew all about that because you went around and erased Palindrome from them, and you drew the heart with Mike in it under the home ec table after I told you that I planned to check the room out. Too bad you missed the one in the gym locker, but that gave you the chance to try to kill me."

I stopped and waited for him to say something. Finally he opened his eyes and turned to me. He was smiling, but the smile didn't fit his face or the look in his eyes. Soundlessly he pretended to clap his hands.

"This is just like you, Lou. You get things partly right, then screw it all up. I did scratch Mike in a heart under Cathy's home ec table. That was just to foul you up because I guessed you were going to pretend to be some kind of hotshot detective. But I didn't erase anything from the top of her desk. Somebody did that before I even thought about it.

"Sure, I used to come here with Cathy, and, can you believe it, she was going to dump me for some retarded garage mechanic. She said that she couldn't do any more for me, that I needed professional help. Her helping me, that's a laugh. I tried to teach her what the world is really like. You need power to get what you want, power and discipline. She couldn't face up to that, so she went and found some dumb slob to help."

Eric moved over closer to me until I could feel his breath on my face. "People don't realize how important discipline is, Lou," he said confidentially, flipping open his cigarette lighter.

The small yellow flame licked upward, and he held it under the palm of his hand.

"Stop!" I shouted.

He continued, staring at me with a fixed smile. That was when I knew he was crazy.

"Stop!" I pulled his hand away from the flame.

"You see, Lou," he said calmly, putting the lighter away with his undamaged hand, "a guy can become whatever he wants if he bosses other people instead of letting them boss him and if he has enough self-discipline. I think you can understand that because, underneath all your sweaty, stinking fear, there is something strong in you. But the world is never going to be perfect like you want it. You have to make it the way you want it to be."

"Did you kill Cathy?"

"No, why should I? There are plenty of girls where she came from, some of them lots prettier. I didn't even hit her, I just walked away."

"And you didn't even tell the police that you had seen her here last. Maybe they could have traced what happened to her if they had known."

"Why should I care what happened to her? Who knows what guy she took up with? That's none of my business."

"And you were scared," I added.

The confident smile slipped. "What have I got to be scared of?" he almost shouted.

"You were afraid the police would suspect you."

"Why should they? I didn't do it, and if you start telling people I did, my mother will have so many lawyers on you it will make your head spin. They'll end up locking you away."

I ignored his tirade. "But that wasn't the worst of it, was it? You were even more afraid that people would find out that you were another of Cathy's injured birds that she tried to nurse. You really couldn't handle that, could you? The big self-reliant superman."

His face got red, and the veins stood out in his neck. For a moment I thought he was going to hit me. Then he gave a funny little smirk and said, "I'm going to treat you the same way I treated her. I'm going to walk away and put you out of my life, loser."

Eighteen

I watched him run away. I believed he hadn't killed Cathy. He was too crazy, if that made any sense. He really couldn't care enough about somebody to want to kill, except as a joke. It was a relief to me that he hadn't done it, but now I was back at the starting point without a good suspect. Of course I could always go to the police and tell them where she had been seen last. An investigation of the area might turn up some valuable clues.

"How's it going, Lou?" someone behind me asked. I turned, and there was Marty Stanton leaning against a tree, watching me. "I'm afraid I overheard your argument with Eric. I hate to throw a monkey wrench into your investigation, but I don't think he did it.''

"Yeah, but, you know, I was just thinking that maybe we can pick up some clues if this area is searched.''

He nodded and sat down across from me where Eric had been. ''Sure, they would dig up this whole clearing searching for evidence or even for the body.''

I shifted uneasily.

"You know, you only screwed up on one piece of this thing. You got the wrong person.''

''What do you mean?''

Marty gazed almost sleepily into the distance. "How old do you think I am?'' he asked.

I shrugged. ''I don't know. Twenty-seven, twenty-eight, what does it matter?''

"It doesn't matter, Lou. You think I'm old, that's the point. Even though I'm only twenty-two, five years older than you, I'm old and you're young.''

"But you're an adult and a cop, so naturally I think of you as being a lot older.''

"Yeah, I guess Cathy did, too. Even though we used to talk a lot at school and I sometimes imagined that maybe she thought of me as somebody around her own age, I guess she never really did.''

He waited for me to say something. I didn't.

"I gave her a ride a couple of times after school and dropped her off across from the gas station. Just out of curiosity I followed her one day and spotted the two of them here. I've had my eye on Eric ever since he showed up at school. I tried to give Cathy a few subtle warnings about him, but she was determined to find a good side to the guy that no one else saw.''

"I guess I saw it, too—at least sometimes," I said.

Marty nodded. "She told me on the day she broke up with Eric that she planned to do it. Eric had turned out to be sicker than Cathy could deal with. I followed her after school because I was afraid he might get violent. I hid in the bushes and heard them argue, the same way I heard you and Eric today.''

He paused and watched me for a moment, as though trying to figure out what my reaction would be to his next sentence. My mouth went dry, and I could feel the muscles in my neck begin to ache with tension.

"After Eric left, I came out of hiding like I did today and tried to comfort her. At first I just put my arm around her because she was crying, then, before either one of us knew what was happening, we were kissing. Maybe I came on a little strong, or she suddenly realized what she was doing. Anyway, she panicked and pulled my gun out of the holster. I got scared and struggled with her to get it back. Somehow it went off.''

"Couldn't you do anything to help her?''

"It was too late.''

"So you hid the body?''

"Buried it. In fact, it's right under that mound you're sitting on.''

Finally I knew where Cathy was. Even though I was scared and nervous, I felt a small rush of relief.

"When people noticed she was missing,'' Marty continued, "I was put in charge of the early stages of the investigation, so I erased all the Palindromes from the desks. It took me a while to find out what that meant,'' he said with a chuckle. "But I was playing the angle that Eric wouldn't volunteer any information, so if I could keep the police from discovering his connection to Cathy, it would be harder for them to link her disappearance to me.'' He shook his head sadly. "I almost made it, except for that damned heart on the gym locker. I never figured on something being there.''

"How did you find out about that?'' I asked.

"I knew Jessie was concerned about Cathy's disappearance because she was always after me for information during the investigation. She had me worried, so I've generally been keeping track of her. Then I started seeing the two of you together and you began to ask me questions about Cathy, so I decided to follow you for a while."

"You smashed the car windshield in the library parking lot and threw that weight in the locker room?"

"Yeah. Sorry about that episode in the gym. I purposely threw it high. I just wanted to discourage the two of you, not kill anybody. But I guess you were both too determined."

"What are you going to do now?" I asked. My heart was beating so hard that it hurt.

"Well, you were right, Lou. If the police find out about this place, they'll discover the body, maybe even the bullet, and even if they don't trace it all to me, I don't think I can go on pretending anymore."

He drew his gun from its holster and leveled it directly at my chest. Then with a quick, graceful motion he flipped the gun around and handed it to me.

"I think you'd better go call your father," he said.

Nineteen

I haven't gotten to the shore yet. I certainly didn't get to go with Eric because his mother sold their house and they left town a few weeks after I saw him last in The Clearing. But I did get to play baseball. For a while I was even a celebrity, and people would come to games just to point me out. Going down the halls at school, kids would whisper that I was the one who had been with Marty before he turned himself in. But after a few weeks it died down, and by June I was back to being a regular kid again.

Jessie and I still get together quite a bit. She's finally forgiven me for not telling her who I suspected; if I had it to do all over again, this time I would tell her.

I'm working this summer, but not at the police station. Under the circumstances, that would have been too tense. I convinced my father, who listens to me a little more these days, that I could get a job on my own, and I finally landed one loading trucks at a warehouse. My body aches, but every day it feels stronger.

I don't worry so much anymore, either. I guess that, once you take a chance, you aren't quite as scared the next time something comes up, and maybe, as Marlowe would say, "That's all you can ask for, kid."

COMING NEXT MONTH
FROM
CROSSWINDS™

TOUGHING IT OUT
by Joan Oppenheimer

Would Jennifer have the strength to shatter the world she had so carefully built around herself? This question will continue to haunt the reader long after she has laid the book aside. A story for today's girls.

CLIFFHANGER
by Glen Ebisch

Lou Dunlop and supercool Jessie are on the trail again— this time it takes them both almost to the edge.

AVAILABLE THIS MONTH

DOES YOUR NOSE GET IN THE WAY, TOO?
Arlene Erlbach

LOU DUNLOP: PRIVATE EYE
Glen Ebisch

LOU DUNLOP STRIKES AGAIN!

More about that "fearless" teen detective and his sexy sidekick, Jessie. This time Jessie is in hot water, and it's up to Lou to bail her out.

"This is the life, Jes, the sun and the water, and nothing to do but enjoy them," I said.

"I'm glad you could come along, Lou. I really didn't think your father would let you. Didn't he say he wanted you to work all summer?"

"Well, I just convinced him that a guy needed a break before starting his senior year in high school. We've got two whole weeks to drown ourselves in pleasure."

"Drown might be an unfortunate expression at the seashore...."

Is Jessie more right than she knows?

Read all about it in *Cliffhanger* by Glen Ebisch, coming in July from Crosswinds.

ATTRACTIVE, SPACE SAVING BOOK RACK

Display your most prized novels on this handsome and sturdy book rack. The hand-rubbed walnut finish will blend into your library decor with quiet elegance, providing a practical organizer for your favorite hard-or soft-covered books.

Only $9.95

Approximately 16" x 8" when assembled

Assembles in seconds!

To order, rush your name, address and zip code, along with a check or money order for $10.70* ($9.95 plus 75¢ postage and handling) payable to *Crosswinds*.

Crosswinds
Book Rack Offer
901 Fuhrmann Blvd.
P.O. Box 1396
Buffalo, NY 14269-1396

Offer not available in Canada.

*New York residents add appropriate sales tax.

BKR-3